Bryce Milligan's interest in his Irish roots began in his teens, when he determined to become a poet and storyteller in the tradition of the Irish *filid*. At the University of Texas, he studied linguistics and language —including Old Irish and Anglo-Saxon.

He is the author of *Daysleepers & Other Poems*, three plays for children, and over 400 articles and book reviews. Along the way, he has been a folksinger, a guitar maker, a bibliographer, a college teacher of English, and (currently), book columnist for the *San Antonio Light*. He and his wife, Mary, have two children: Michael and Brigid Aileen.

# With the Wind, Kevin Dolan

Tom and his younger brother Kevin leave Ireland for Texas in 1835, smarting under the latest English injustices. They have never known much beyond their home village and their bitterness against England. Now they experience Liverpool, a sea voyage, shipwreck, and cholera, and the bustling city of New Orleans. Arriving finally in Texas, they find new hardships —snakes, alligators, hostile Comanches—and make unexpected friends. On the eve of the Texian Revolution, Kevin learns that the difference between oppressor and oppressed is not so clear when life, land, and liberty are at stake.

# With the Wind, Kevin Dolan

## A Novel of Ireland and Texas

by
## Bryce Milligan

Illustrations by Paul Hudgins

Corona Publishing Company     San Antonio     1987

ISBN Number 0-931722-44-6 (cloth)
0-931722-45-4 (paper)
Library of Congress Catalog Number
86-70018

Designed by Paul Hudgins

*Printed and bound in the United States of America*

Dedicated, as always,
to my wife
*Mary Frances Guerrero Milligan*
and our young readers
*Michael and Brigid Aileen*

# Acknowledgements

I would like to thank Professor Ruth Lehmann, University of Texas at Austin, scholar and poet, for educating the Irish already in my blood. Thanks also go to James Delaney and the Ancient Order of Hibernians for a grant which allowed this novel to go forward when it was languishing; to John Brendan Flannery for reading portions of the manuscript and offering many helpful suggestions; to Mary Osborn and Jo Myler of the San Antonio Public Library for always finding answers when needed; to Tom Shelton and Debbie Large of the Institute of Texan Cultures Library for their expertise and constant interest; to Mimi Quintanilla, Holly Morton, and Sarah Kerr of the Witte Memorial Museum; to David Bowen of Corona Publishing Company for years of encouragement; to Isabeth Hardy for being a true patron of the arts and artists; to Samuel Milligan for help on the New Orleans section as well as unwittingly instigating much of this; and to my wife, Mary, my best critic and the source of many ideas, including this book.

# Author's Note

As in every historical fiction, there is some concern among readers as to just what is history and what is fiction. In *With the Wind, Kevin Dolan,* almost every "event" in the story is based upon the historical facts of the establishment of the Power Colony near Refugio, Texas, in 1834. Ship names, family names, dates, and characters such as James Power, Captain Coppin, Commissioner Vidauri, even Karankawa Tom, are all represented faithfully. Tom and Kevin Dolan, the Donohues, Owen Morgan, and Brian Ruadh O'Mallory are all "made up," but they include bits and pieces of many of the actual immigrants as they are mentioned in sources such as the memoirs of Rosalie Priour, on file at the Institute of Texan Cultures in San Antonio.

Much of the novel consists of dialogue. This conversational approach is intended to give the flavor of oral history. Much of Ireland's history as well as that of the early immigrants to Texas was conveyed by oral means before it came to be written down. It should be mentioned that the dialect spoken by the Irish characters in this book is a much-watered-down version of that found in County Wexford. If the dialect had been preserved intact, it would have been as difficult for modern readers as is, for example, the original *Uncle Remus* by Joel Chandler Harris. Lest the difference between the conversational and narrative portions of this text be too great, I have opted for an informal prose style which often bends the rules of "the King's English."

My own Irish forbears, incidentally, were not part of this story. Old John Milligan left his hometown of Dublin around 1810 and made his way to Lexington, Ohio. It took three generations more for the family to reach Texas.

I would hope, however, that *With the Wind, Kevin Dolan* is more than just another adventurous tale of immigration to the United States. Kevin's dilemma is one we should all share.

—Bryce Milligan

# Contents

# Part One

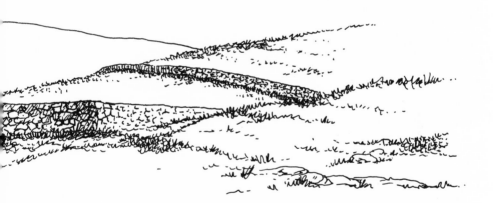

*Chapter 1*

# A Change of Dreams

"It was Brian O'Mallory put him up to it," said Kevin Dolan of his older brother, Tom. "My Da says it will give time to the men at Mr. Donohue's place, but I'll wager it's to be showing off his great courage for Mary O'Reilly that's got himself out here in the cold dawn."

The boys giggled at that like a lot of girls at a party—too young to dance and too old to play hurly—but Kevin shushed them. "Quiet now, or you'll have the redcoats down on Tommy lad. So shisht and keep an eye out."

Just then Tom Dolan came running around the end of the fence. He crouched low, turning to look back, then came up to the group of younger boys. "Is it anything you've seen moving in the yard, Kevin?" he asked.

"No, Tommy, it's quiet as a mouse you were this night."

"Come on then, lads," said Tom, "this'll be no safe place for the likes of us in these few minutes." Leading them into an alley, then down a narrow street, then up

another alley, Tom brought them to the opposite side of
the small square where the English soldiers would mount
up for their patrol at dawn. They hid behind a number of
rum barrels blocking the entrance to the alley.

"And what was it you did to the dirty Brits' horses?"
asked Owen, a ten-year-old boy from the village.

"Why, nothing at all to their horses," said Tom. "I wouldn't be for harming an innocent animal even if it is in the King's employ. I slit halfway through all their saddle cinches. It's a royal show we'll be having when they start to ride out."

And a royal show it was. When the dawn was full and the morning patrol of fifteen redcoats had led out their horses and saddled up, the fat Major gave the order to mount. He was the first to go down. Halfway into the saddle, the straps broke and, stiff as a board—still holding the saddle between his legs—the Major spun off the horse and landed on his head. Some of the soldiers got upright before wheeling off the other side of their horses, but all went down at last. Several of the horses bolted off through the streets and there was a great deal of confusion as soldiers ran this way and that trying to catch their mounts and looking for someone to blame. It was a good thing that they were so noisy about it as the boys could hardly keep from breaking into laughter themselves. Then, one by one, silent and unseen, the Irish lads slipped away and went home, feeling much the better for a good joke on the British.

Kevin was as proud of Tom as if his brother had led some great attack on a British fort. But Tom, who was eighteen and knew better, said, "It was a darn fool thing to do, Kevin, and don't you be letting me catch you fooling around like that."

"Oh, Tom, you're a hero this day but you don't have to start telling *me* how dangerous it was. I'm twelve already. I could have helped you this morning if only Ma hadn't made me swear to stay out of the British stables."

"And I'd have had as much trouble keeping you quiet as I did the horses. Go on, it's like you just said—you're only twelve."

Kevin stamped down the narrow boreen, trying to make the curious pointed-toe footprints that could only be made when the dust in the lane was half dry and half damp from the morning dew.

"Why couldn't we just call in some rebels, the Defenders or the United Irishmen? They'd set those soldiers down but hard! Maybe even blow up their barracks," said Kevin, waving his hands in imitation of the explosion.

"That wasn't the point of this morning's doings. If we'd called on some rebel group, they would sure have killed a soldier or two and then all of County Wexford would have had to pay for a year and beyond. Da said only to slow them up this morning so the men over at Donohue's farm could finish moving their grain before the soldiers brought round the tax man. It's all night our neighbors will have been working, and they'll be needing a little daylight to be after covering their tracks."

"And would the English be for taking it all, do you think?" asked Kevin.

"All and more, if they could," said Tom, "especially since last year's harvest was so poor. Father says that Mr. Donohue talked them into an extension last year, so it's two years' taxes with interest he'll be owing now. The English mean to tax him off his land, so they'll be taking it all for sure. If the men got half the grain moved last night into the neighbors' barns, then the Brits can only take what they find. 'Tis certain they wouldn't know a good crop from a bad one these days and in this part of the country—especially with something like grain when everyone around here raises potatoes. That's why Mr. Donohue planted all grain this year so that the English wouldn't know how much to expect. It would be a fine thing though if God would send some rain to wash out the wagon tracks this morning."

Tom and Kevin had left the village and were coming to the top of the hill overlooking their farm. At the top of the hill stood a stone cross. To Kevin, this was about the most special place on earth—except maybe Tara Hill in County Meath, far north where the old kings of Ireland had sat. Father O'Flaherty had once told Kevin that this cross was over a thousand years old. You could still see the pictures of the saints carved deep into the stone, and you could pick out Saint Peter from his staff and keys. Mostly, though, the cross was covered with swirling interlaced designs. Kevin had spent many afternoons tracing them out, only to find that it was all one line laced together.

"Let's stop at the cross," said Kevin, "and pray for rain."

Tom looked up at the cloudless morning sky. "You can't be asking God for too much, Kevin. If it had rained last night, they couldn't have moved the grain. Still, it wouldn't hurt now to be saying a prayer at all, no matter what it's for. We know the redcoats will be coming, and none too happy after this morning's games."

At the stone cross, they said three Ave Marias and one Pater Noster out loud together. Kevin prayed for rain; Tom did not say what he prayed for. From the top of the hill, they could see part of the road leading out of the village. The British had not set out yet. Soon the boys were off and running down the hill, jumping and rolling in the long grass until they came to the prickly furze and the low stone wall that was the northern edge of their father's main field of potatoes. As they walked across the field to their low cottage of stone, sod, and thatch, their mother came out to call them in for breakfast. Hot tea and bowls of steaming oatmeal porridge were on the table. Father was already smoking his pipe. From that the boys could tell that either he was very worried or else he hadn't yet been to bed, or both.

"And how did it go, Tom?" asked Father. "Do you think you slowed themselves up that much?"

"That he did," broke out Kevin, his mouth full of the hot cereal. "And it's a hero he'll be around here for a while. Mr. O'Mallory's idea worked like a poet's curse. And the fat Major was the first to go down—it was a pinwheel blade he looked like, burying his bonnet in the grass that way."

"Well, it's a hard time they'll have of it, trying to find a saddle worth sitting in their stable this day," said Tom. "I cut every cinch and harness strap in the place."

"Well, it's worried sick we were all night, but it sounds a fine piece of work. You're sure now, you weren't seen?"

"Sure and we weren't," said Tom, "and we were out of the village before they'd even caught their horses."

While Tom and Kevin finished their breakfasts, their father told them how his night had gone. The neighbors had all gathered after dark and loaded six loads of grain into Mr. Donohue's wagon. Each load had been taken to a different neighbor's grain shed, or just dumped on the ground and covered with blankets and thatch mats if they had no shed to put it in.

"It's a lucky thing that Donohue's barn has such a stoney path from itself to the boreen. The wagon didn't make such a mess of tracks that way. And sure you'd think the road itself was your Ma's floor—that clean it was when we finished sweeping it with branches this morning."

"Six times it was," said Ma, "your Da drove that wagon out into the black night, and we women brewing tea enough for all the heroes of Tara. Faith, was more tea drunk last night in County Wexford than the Americans threw in Boston harbor."

"Donohue's harvest was better than we expected, to spare six loads out of it," said Tom.

"Aye," put in Ma, "and them leaving more than half of it there and Mrs. Donohue saying that by rights we ought to foul what was left except the redcoats wouldn't take it for the taxes and how they might not be fooled anyway. Ah, sure 'twill be more than that woman can stand. And them thinking if they can keep the farm past this year's round of taxes, they'll sell it and get off to the Americas."

"They'll be going to the Americas, did you say?" asked Kevin.

"It's what Mrs. Donohue was at telling us all last night" said Ma. "There be a man down in Ballygarrett, a Mr. Power, who's been gone from Eire these twenty years and more, and it's the land of Texas he's talking up."

Tom gave a laugh. "And what would the likes of old Donohue be good for in a heathen land like that?" he asked.

"To be finding a husband for their Rose," laughed Kevin.

"And you be holding your tongue of such things,"

said Father. "Rose is not as comely as some, but she's a fine-hearted woman. And Texas is neither a heathen land nor Protestant, but a fair brave Catholic country so they say."

"And how would you be knowing such things, Mr. Dolan?" asked Ma. "It's not a man of the wide world you are."

"To be sure, I heard your Mr. Power talking up his new land the same time Mr. Donohue did."

"And you were thinking we wouldn't be interested, were you?" chided Ma. "Well, I know it's not you who's thinking of sailing away. The Donohues, now, they have their reasons. Isn't he the only son of Eire in these parts still owns his own land, and hasn't it shrunk like a raisin from the days of old? And what a pain it is to Mr. Donohue himself to be able to see the chimney smoke over the hills from the manor house that was built by his own great-great-grandfather? They know that the English mean to tax the land itself away from them. It may be they can make their fortune in this Texas and come back to Ireland in better times. Mrs. Donohue says . . ."

"All right, Ma," broke in Father, "all I can say is that no redcoated Protestant Englishman has the right to take a man's harvest and not leave him anything to eat nor plant. What we did last night we did for love of justice and a fellow Gael—not to be sending Rose and Margaret and Patrick Eamonn Donohue off to be pioneers, though it might be a good thing for us all in the end."

"And what might you be meaning by that now, Mr. Dolan?" asked Ma. "Is it glad you are to be losing your best friend?"

"To tell you God's own truth, I was considering—just mulling it over, mind you—considering the idea of sending young Tom here with them on the boat to Texas."

"Mother of God, have mercy on us," said Ma as she crumpled down on a stool. "That's a wild hare scheme for a mother to hear of, you sending off her second son to be drowned in the wide ocean or killed by red Indians."

Tom was just as taken aback by the suggestion as was his mother, but he did not say anything. It was not that he wanted or did not want to go, but rather that he had been wishing and dreaming that he had enough money to marry Mary O'Reilly *and* move to America. Tom knew that the redcoats could push them past their ability to pay their taxes and the required Protestant tithe, and that any year now a failure of the potato crop could deprive them of their home and livelihood. Living on the edge was like that, and it had happened to many families all over Ireland.

"Father," Tom said, "how much does it cost to buy passage on Mr. Power's boat to Texas? Did he tell you that much?"

"It costs eight pounds sterling, and you must be taking a year's supply of food for the journey, and tools and a plow."

"It's a mountain of silver money to be sure," said Tom, "but we could make a new plow all right. Is that it?"

"No, faith," chuckled Father, "you need the luck of a bale of shamrocks and the blessings of all the saints."

Mother was a bit recovered now, and said, "And where would you be getting eight pounds sterling money now, Mr. Dolan? Sure you haven't been hiding it all these twenty-two years since I took you for better or worse in

Saint Clare's church."

"No, it's no money I've got hidden away, but a bit of luck. Patrick Donohue is in the way of owing me a great favor for saving his Timothy from drowning when he was but a wee lad—God rest his soul but he didn't live two years after that to be run down by a jaunting car. But Mr. Donohue tells me that he'll be paying Tommy's passage, food and all, if Tommy would agree to work for him for a year after they got their land in Texas."

"And what was it you told him, Da?" asked Tom.

"I told him I'd be asking you to think on it when I was done thinking on it myself. It's quite a while yet before Mr. Power will be taking ship."

Kevin could not make up his mind whether this was the best or the worst news he had ever heard. Of course Tom would go to America. Who could pass up such an offer when the only thing holding him back was Mary O'Reilly? But Tom was everything to Kevin. It was Tom who had taught Kevin to cut peat and tend sheep and milk cows and tie knots and, well, everything. Together they had gone hunting and roaming and playing such tricks on their neighbors and on the British as they could manage.

The only thing that could ever keep them apart was Mary. Kevin did not understand that at all. She was a fine girl, and Kevin could remember a time when she had been ready enough to take a tumble in a game of hurly when no one was looking. But she had gotten pretty—beautiful according to Tom—and the boys had stopped playing with her. Kevin had to admit that even he liked to look at her, especially when she wore her long curly auburn hair loose. And Kevin was no fool—he could see that she had a good figure as well as Tom could. But now Tom seemed to change whenever they saw her. He would take off his hat even if she was just packing a load of peat down an empty lane. Then Tom would offer to carry her pack and they would take the longest way home. Sometimes Tom even told Kevin to go home when they met her. It seemed to Kevin that he had as much to say to Mary as Tom did, but he would go on and run over the fields and try to forget it.

"Sure it wasn't that way with Michael," thought Kevin. One day their oldest brother had walked in and said that he was going to marry Peggy Mahon. They had taken up on a bit of land two miles south and that was that. Now they had little Stephen, named for Kevin's father, and Peggy was pregnant again.

"Love's a thing not in my understanding," thought Kevin as he listened to the family discussing Tom's journey to come. "First it can make the ancient heroes do the strangest things, and now it makes brothers walk home by different lanes. And now this. It's breaking my heart will be if Tom goes off and leaves me here, but he'd be leaving me anyway once he got married. Still, I'd not be that much happier leaving Ma and Da and Brigid and little Cathleen and Michael's new family to go off with Tom to Texas."

"Kevin, your Da's after asking you a question," said Ma in a loud voice.

"I'm sorry, Da," he said, "I wasn't hearing you."

"Dreaming of Texas himself, he was, I'll be bound," put in Ma.

"And rightly so. It's no use saying there's a future here in Eire for him. He'll only be poorer than we are the way things are going. But what it was that I was asking, Kevin, was what you'd be thinking of going off with your brother."

"To Texas itself?" asked Kevin.

"No and to be sure," said Ma, "to Glencolumbkille to pray the English away. To Texas sure, lad. I'll not be sending out one of my boys into the world without someone to look after him."

That was Ma's kind of logic. She would not send one because the dangers were so great, but she would send two because the Lord would not grieve her so by letting her lose them both.

"But Da," said Kevin, feeling very shaken all at once, "how will you be running the farm at all without Tom and myself?"

"Ah boy, there's no use breaking a shin on a stool that's not in your way. It's not as if one cow, a few sheep, and a few patches of potatoes is more than your old Da can look after," said Father laughing. "But I thank you for the thinking of it."

"Your father made this place what it is out of a field of nothing but rocks and gorse before you came along," said Ma.

"But there's still rocks to be pulled out, and who'll be cutting the peat and dragging it back over two miles of hills —or worse, down five miles of lanes as crooked as a Belfast parson and themselves so narrow that Timothy Donohue couldn't stand clear of an Englishman in a jaunting car? And there's shearing in the spring . . ." Kevin couldn't find it in himself to go on, because the thought of doing all those things without Tom beside him was a lonely thought indeed.

"I can cut the peat, Kevin," said his sister Brigid. "And

it's a sackful I can bring home every day on my way home from school. It's often enough I've walked beside you that length over the hills and you doing all the carrying."

"You're not but a slip of a girl, Brigid," said Kevin.

At that, Brigid hit him squarely in the middle of the forehead with a ball of wool yarn she had been rolling. "I'll be as old as you are in two years' time, Kevin Dolan. It's only twelve you are now, and you bringing the peat home from school the same way since you were seven. Besides, you'll be sending us bushels of money in no time. We can hire an English lord to be delivering us fuel to the cottage door."

"Shisht," said Father, "and isn't it a sad thing to be talking about your two brothers, leaving in that way. We'll be missing you every minute of every day, you and Tommy, and sure it is the good Lord will get tired of hearing your names in our prayers. But the truth of things is, that if the landlord should put the rent up for auction, or the Protestant tithe should go up, curse it, or a bad crop come along, it's out on the lanes we'd be like gypsies. We'd have to move in on Michael and Pegeen, and them with barely enough land to raise a decent crop of potatoes, to say nothing of grazing a cow for milk for the baby that's to come. It's another hope we'd have with you and Tom making your fortunes in Texas. If worse came to worst, there'd be that chance we could all come along and join you in Texas."

"What?" said Ma. "Is it the whole family you'd be putting on the wide ocean now, Mr. Dolan? This Texas has gotten into your brain for sure."

"It's coming back to Ireland with our fortunes in our

pockets I was thinking, Da," said Tom.

"Oh, aye, I love Eire as well as any," said Father, "but it's many a long year it'll be before we're well rid of the English and their burdens. There'll be no way for an Irishman to rise in Ireland for a long time. But look at the chances in America. Why, the President of the United States now, a Mr. Andrew Jackson, is the son of a man Ulster born."

"True enough, Da," said Tom, "and a grand foe of the English he was in his early years, but it's not to the likes of the United States we'll be going."

"But it's a brave free land, Tom, and you can perhaps be making your own country soon."

"Mercy," said Ma. "It's not even on the boat they are and you telling them to start a revolution. Sure it is that an Irishman's never happy but when he's fighting. I'll have no more of such talk. If you two boys go to that far land, it's to be building up farms and good homes, not a new country."

"And while you're at that, we'll be having two less mouths to feed," Brigid teased.

"Shisht, girl," said Ma.

But Kevin knew that Brigid did not mean it so harshly. He knew how she felt about her brothers, and that she would be as lonely without them as he would be without Tom. "It's not that I don't want to be going and doing grand things," said Kevin. "It's just that leaving all of you is like the cutting out of my heart. But 'tis the same with letting Tommy go off by himself. It's destroyed I'll be either way."

Father came over and laid his hand on Kevin's shoulder. "Well, it's not today you'll be going for sure. We still have to see whether the British tax man accepts Mr. Donohue's grain harvest as payment on the two years of taxes and his interest and all. If Mr. Donohue's not to go, then sure no one else will be going, at least not from this family. Even if it all turns out fine with Patrick, Tommy here has yet to say whether he'd be for taking up Mr. Donohue's offer."

Kevin looked at Tom. "Is that right then? Would you be thinking of not going at all?"

"Sure and it's a hard decision," said Tom. "I need to think on it a good deal and . . ."

"And you'll be needing a good long talk with that Mary O'Reilly," said Brigid with a mischievous grin.

"That's true enough," said Tom, glad to have it in the open. "It's often we've dreamed of going to America together, but we were thinking more of going to the civilized part of the country to the north. That's if we could make the fare at any time. We never thought of it being myself who'd go off alone—and we never even thought of Texas but as a wild place."

"At least it's a Catholic country you'd be going to instead of to that land of blaspheming Protestants. Whether or no they beat down the British, the United States is definitely Protestant," said Ma. "I hear that Our Lady, the Virgin Mary, has even appeared in Mexico. Father O'Flaherty heard all about it from a Spanish priest when he was in Dublin last."

"I don't know about the Virgin being seen in Mexico," said Father, "but your Ma is right that you'd be better off in Texas. I'm sure Mary O'Reilly will be agreeing with her once she gets it all thought out. Besides, you'd need more money to settle well in the United States than you'd ever

be able to take out of Eire. Sure you'd be poorer than we are here."

"And where would you have been hearing such a tale as that?" asked Tom. "Everyone says there's plenty of land to be had in the United States. I never heard of anyone being poor there."

"I heard it from this Mr. Power," said Father. "He seems to know both lands well, and he says that the public lands in the United States cost nearly eight shillings an acre. To be getting free land, you'd have to be travelling as much as 500 miles or more inland. It's no use going to the goat's house to look for wool. Once you're in Texas, the government of Mexico will give you 177 acres to farm. And Mr. Power says that if you start raising cattle, they'll give you upwards of 4,000 acres. He showed it to us in writing."

The family stared at Father. Their own farm wasn't more than thirty acres. Mr. Donohue didn't own more than a hundred. That one man could actually own over 4,000 acres of land anywhere on earth was staggering.

"Hoo now and there's a hole in that promise for sure," said Ma. "And what under God's blue sky could one man even do with so much land?"

"Well, the catch is that you have to get a herd of cattle together before you can get the land," said Father, "or at least show that you have the money to do it."

"Well, if it's nothing more than that," Ma grinned at Tom, "it looks like you'll have to stick to being a farmer, Tommy."

"And myself," said Kevin.

"And yourself," said Father. "But it's a brave fair land they'll be going to, Ma, where you get what your wits will earn you. Mr. Power says that you can still go out into the wilderness and round up wild horses, or trade blankets and such to the Indians for horses. You can build up stock that way."

"I knew 'twas into the wilderness you'd be sending them, out among the savages who'd kill a man for his coat," wailed Ma.

"Ah, Ma," said Tom, "sure it's better than being hanged in Dublin city for being Irish in Ireland. But I still need to be thinking on it for a few days."

"That's only right. You boys go and think it over for a while," said Father. "We'll be talking about it for longer than it takes for you to make up your minds, I'll wager. Now get along, and be back in time for supper."

*Chapter 2*

# Texas?

Kevin and Tom walked back up the hill. There was no doubt in Kevin's mind that they would not walk up this hill many more times. November was well on them now, and the long grass was honey gold. A wind was stirring out of the southwest and the grass rustled softly as it bent to the breeze. You could see a green sort of sheen as the longer blades of grass moved to reveal what grew closer to the earth. Looking across the land, the hills seemed to be vibrating with the changing colors. By the time they came to the stone cross, the wind had risen a good deal and turned definitely colder. The boys had not spoken.

"You'll be off to see Mary now?" asked Kevin.

"Aye," said Tom, standing with his back to the cross and looking east toward the sea.

Kevin watched Tom for a while, then turned to see what it was he was looking at. There was nothing—only the next hill, and then another, flickering with the wind from green to brown and back again. Far away, Kevin could see the darker color on the horizon which was the ocean. "Brian O'Mallory," said Kevin, "says that the fair folk are forever desiring to be going into the sea to a land beneath the waters. He says that the less we believe in them, the more they want to go into the sea and never set foot in Eire again."

"Mr. O'Mallory's after telling tales all the time," said Tom, not turning around.

"Well, it's that lonesome I'd be if you were to go off to America without me, but it's destroyed I'll be to be quitting Eire," said Kevin. "It's only for the chance of coming back in a grand style that I'll be going."

"And don't you think I'll be missing the Island at all? To say nothing of Ma and Da and Michael and the children?"

"And Mary?" added Kevin.

"Aye, and Mary," said Tom. "It's a hard thing and no doubt to be leaving everything you love to be stravaging off to a new land where a boreen will look like a king's highway, but I can't find the sense of not going. Da's right enough—there'll be no future here for the likes of us. But it's a queer hard thing to be forced out of your own land just because the soldiery and politicians of another land won't let it prosper the way it would on its own. I'll not be coming back to Eire unless it's to be fetching Mary or bringing money to Ma and Da."

"I'll not be coming back unless it's with a gun in my hand to be driving the English off this island," said Kevin. "But I'm thinking that it's not in our time that the English will be driven off so. As much as Ireland would like to throw off the British, they've made us too poor to raise a proper rebellion. I don't know, Tommy, I don't know what's best for Ma and Da, or for Ireland, or for you and Mary, or for me."

"Well, it's no more befuddled you are than myself," laughed Tom. "I wouldn't be going off without you, though," he said putting an arm on Kevin's shoulder. "We're a pretty fair team at farm work and hunting and such, even if you don't understand the girls at all. But it's Mary I'd best be talking to now, for if she's not for sending me off with a great will, it's not over the sea I'll be going. Will you be staying here for a while, or where at all?"

"It's hard thinking, and hard waiting I'll be doing while you're off deciding our fate," said Kevin. "If you're to be going, then I'll be beside you. But sure they wouldn't be sending me off without you, nor would I be wanting to be making such a journey. So get off to your fair colleen and find out whether it's on the sea we'll be throwing our fates. I'll be here unless the soldiers come stirring up trouble about the grain."

"I'd almost forgotten about that adventure," said Tom. "Perhaps I'd better not be going off to see Mary today."

"Go on with you," said Kevin. "What is it at all you'd be doing, even if the scoundrels raise trouble? Isn't that the very thing driving us to Texas?"

"Sure and it is, little brother," said Tom. "I'll be back as soon as ever Mary will let me go."

Kevin watched his brother walk north down the back side of the hill. Tom climbed over the small stone wall and disappeared down the boreen leading to the village. The O'Reilly family lived just beyond the small gathering of shops, almost in the shadow of the redcoats' stables. Their small house was at the head of a glen that ran between two of the foothills of the higher hills beyond Gorey. If you followed that glen north, and then followed the coast for about ten miles, you would come to a tall hill called Tara, named in memory of a higher hill, the seat of the kings to the north. From the top of the southern Tara you could look out over the ocean and watch the schooners and packet ships plying their way up the coast from Wexford. A little farther north, the ships would turn away east to cross the Irish Sea to reach Liverpool in England.

Kevin wondered if he and Tom would have to go to Liverpool before leaving for Texas. Da said that most of the ships crossing the Atlantic left from the port of Liverpool. It made Kevin angry that even in leaving Ireland, which they were only doing because of the English injustice, they would have to go to England before leaving for Texas. Liverpool was a place, Father O'Flaherty had said once, "full of evil men and worse women." It sounded ominous to Kevin. He had heard many tales of Irish emigrants having to return home instead of sailing off to a new land, penniless after having been cheated out of what little they had. "But sure it's like the English to be making as much money as they can, even if it's from splitting up families and such," Kevin thought to himself. He determined that he would trust no one, bishop or barmaid, when they got on English soil.

Kevin did not want to go, but he was beginning to see the necessity of it. "Da's right," Kevin said out loud to the cross. "If there's a chance across the ocean, then we must take it. Staying here, it would only be the same thing over

again. Hasn't every family in County Wexford its martyrs
from the 1798 rebellion? Little good that came of that. Isn't
my own sister, Brigid Elizabeth, named for my grand-
mother that died on an English gibbet for walloping a
redcoat with a frying pan, and himself stealing her cow?"

The cross did not reply, but Kevin knew that it had
seen a good deal more suffering in its thousand years in
this spot than Kevin had even heard of. It was on this very
hill that four children from the village of Killenagh had
been bayoneted to death by a company of Protestant
yeomen out of the north in the English pay. "Ah, it could
have been so glorious," he said to the cross, "and didn't
we make those yeomen pay—there wasn't one of them
left alive after their meeting with the pitchforks of the
Boolavogue farmers." But it had not been glorious at all.
Poverty made men weak, even Irishmen, and treason was
well paid. Before the rebellion had even begun, over thirty
of its Irish leaders, some of them great lords, had been
betrayed and hanged.

The country was in no better state now in 1833. After
hosting the redcoats' revenge for thirty-five years, Ireland
was even poorer. There were no leaders now like Lord
Edward Fitzgerald, or Wolfe Tone who slit his own throat
rather than let the English have the satisfaction of hanging
him. There was no longer a French army to threaten England; Napoleon's defeat at Waterloo had been as much a
disaster for Ireland as it had been for the French.

Kevin leaned against the cross, feeling the cool stone,
tracing the familiar designs with his finger. "Sure, it's hope-
less we are," thought Kevin. But nagging at the back of his
mind was a half-formed idea. Father had said that the

parents of the American President had been born in Ireland. Everyone knew that President Jackson was the hero who had defeated the British at New Orleans. New Orleans was near Texas. Maybe there were lots of people in that part of the world who hated the British. Maybe if Tom and he worked very hard and became very rich, they could get a whole army together and sail back to free Ireland. But where would they get ships? He could turn pirate for a while like Jean Lafitte, and capture British ships. Or maybe he, Kevin Brendan Dolan, could become a famous Indian fighter like Andrew Jackson, and then rise high in the American government—so high that he could make the American Parliament or Congress or whatever they called it see that Ireland was worse off under the British than America had ever been.

Kevin was dreaming full sail now, seeing himself first as a frontier Indian fighter, then leading an armada of American ships of the line back across the Atlantic. In the '98 rebellion, the French had come to the aid of the Irish by sending a 1,000 man army to the beleaguered island. They had beaten an English army of 3,000 so badly that the hasty English retreat had become known as "the races of Castlebar." The French had come too late to revive the rebellion after the initial shock of losing so many leaders through betrayal. But they had marched on, to the middle of the island, before they had to surrender. That only happened when they were outnumbered twenty to one. "What could be done," Kevin thought, "with a force of 10,000 American soldiers in a well-organized campaign?" But reality broke in when Kevin felt the first few drops of rain.

Looking up, he was surprised to find that it was already mid-afternoon. He had been dreaming beside the cross for nearly five hours. A curtain of rain was rushing up from the Atlantic and would soon be upon him. "Hoo now and aren't you the dreamer," he said to himself. Kevin was a thin boy, with a highwayman's mask of freckles and a shock of unruly light brown hair. "I haven't the look of a hero about me at all," he said to the cross, "but perhaps it'll be growing on me with the hard work of pioneering."

Just then he heard Tom's "halloo" from the lane behind the hill. Tom was just leaping over the wall and began to trot up the hill. Kevin waited until Tom was nearly to the top.

"What is it we're to be, Tommy," he shouted over the wind, "Irish tinkers or frontiersmen?"

"You'll be calling Texas home before Easter next," Tom shouted back. He reached the top of the hill slightly out of breath. "And isn't it the patient one you are today, waiting this length of time for your brother, and the wind about to blow you across the wide sea with no boat at all? Come on now, let's get ourselves home before we're wet through."

Together, they ran down the hill, leaning into the wind sweeping up against them, feeling at each jump that they hung in the air just a moment longer than gravity wanted them to. Just as they reached the bottom, Kevin tripped and rolled onto his brother's legs. Tom went down too, and they wrestled the rest of the way until Kevin rolled over a thistle branch. "Yeow!" he shouted, and stopped to pull the thorny twigs away from the back side of his pants. Tom stood, leaning over with his hands on his knees, laughing at Kevin's predicament.

"And why was it you tripped me into the wet grass?" Tom asked, laughing and gasping for breath. "Wasn't it wet enough we were with the rain?"

"Ah, truth was I fell. I didn't mean to be tripping you."

"A likely tale Ma will say," said Tom. "She'll be scolding us for an hour."

"Well, at least as long as it takes to sew up my pants," said Kevin.

Ma made tea for them, but weaker this time because she was using the same tea leaves she had brewed that morning. They took off their wet clothes and hung them by the peat fire to dry. The fire glowed with a dull red flame over a bed of white ash as fine as a great lady's face powder. The wind outside began to howl and the grey-white smoke from the fire followed the draft quickly up to the central smoke hole of the cottage. Tom changed into his work clothes, but Kevin had to stand near the fire wrapped in a blanket until his only pair of pants had dried.

"We saw you come tumbling down the hill," said Ma. "You must be in high spirits to go wrestling in the rain that way. So tell us, Tommy, what was it that your Mary was saying to you?"

"To tell the truth of it, she was so glad over the thing that at first I thought that all she wanted in the world was to be well rid of me. But then she gave me such a promise to wait until I came fetching her, or just to come whenever I sent her word, that I was surely torn up wondering at her great love for me. Sure she's the finest girl in the world."

"And what a thing to be saying with your own dear sister standing near," said Brigid.

Tom reached out and tousled her strawberry blond hair. "You know I wasn't comparing you," said Tom. "There's no colleen in Ireland to compare with you."

"That's a fine thing to be saying," teased Brigid, "but I'll wager you'll be after sending for Mary O'Reilly before I see aught of a passage to Texas for myself."

"As is only natural," said Father. "Quit your teasing now, Brigid, and don't be adding to the burdens your brother is already carrying." To Tom he said, "So, she thinks she can let you loose for a while, does she?"

"That's right, Da. With a great will and a good heart. Isn't she after telling me that she wouldn't be expecting to hear a word from me for at least a year? She was saying, just like you, Ma, 'If it's a Catholic land, Tommy dear, then you'll be safe enough. The Spanish say their Mass in Latin same as we be saying it.' She thinks that anyone who has the Gaelic and English, and their catechism in Latin, should sure be able to pick up enough Spanish to get around with. I'm no great hand at the languages though."

"Kevin Brendan is," said Brigid. "The schoolmaster is forever saying how he never had a student so quick with English as Kevin."

"It's only to be cursing the redcoats in their own tongue," apologized Kevin. The schoolmaster's praise had gotten him into more than one fight with the neighbor boys. Still, Kevin missed going to school. They could only afford to send one of the children at a time, though, and Kevin had gone on two years longer than Tom.

"I'm glad now we made you go that extra length of schooling, for it's a great use you'll be making of your learning out in Texas," said Father. "You'll have to be doing most of the figuring since Tommy's weak in that, and there'll be a lot of figuring to be done with much land under your hand. We all know you've got more brains about you than you let on, wrestling your brother in the rain for the love of the saints, and we'll be expecting you to be putting them to good use. You let Tommy be doing the heavy work while you learn as much as you can about the place you'll be calling home. Mr. Donohue won't be needing you so much as Tom, so you can scout out the best piece of land to be found for yourselves. But above all, you be for making friends among the folk who already live there. You'll be needing friends for a while as much as you'll be needing seed and rain."

"But don't be letting it get into your head, little brother," said Tom with a grin, "that I won't be putting you behind a plow every now and then."

All this made Kevin feel quite proud. It would be his responsibility to do the financial figuring, and the planning in general when they got to Texas, as well as to learn the language and ways of the Texans. Father had said so. Maybe at the same time he could learn all about Indian fighting and soldiering, but then that's probably what they *didn't* want him doing. Tom was always telling him that he was too young to do this or that, just like when he and Ma had made him promise to stay out of the Brits' stables. "I'll show Tom I know which end of a rifle is which," he thought. "And we'll just see who gets stuck with a plow and a log book."

Out loud, he said, "It's proud I'll be to be doing anything with Tom, even if it's just cutting timber or moving stones. Whatever it is, I'll be giving it my best."

Tom clapped him on the back. "I know you will," he said. "But if this rain is any proof of the power of your prayers, maybe I ought to have you saying rosaries for crops instead of having you planting them. Sure it is," said Tom turning to Father, "there was no sign of rain this morning, but Kevin had us pray for rain up by the cross— to wash out your wagon tracks before the soldiers came. And sure there won't be any tracks to follow after this is over."

The rain was indeed coming down in great sheets now, driven by gusts of wind that smelled of the salt ocean. It made the rock weights that held down the rope netting over their thatch roof clunk dully against the plastered sod walls. It was a comforting sound.

Soon Kevin's clothes were dry and mended, and he sat down to watch the rain and dream of sailing to Texas, and back. With the smell of Father's clay pipe mingling with the fresh sea air, Kevin fell into a peaceful sleep.

## Chapter 3

# A Spoiled *Ceili*

It had been three weeks since Kevin's brother had cut the redcoats' saddle cinches. The soldiers and the tax man had come the day after the rain stopped and taken all the grain they could find—along with some of Mr. Dono-hue's livestock. Evidently, they had not suspected the trick that had been played on them, so Mr. Donohue was in no danger of being charged with anything. Since Mr. Donohue was now supposed by the English to have no crops to sell, it was impossible for him to sell the grain that had been removed to the neighbors' barns and sheds, so he gave it outright to the farmers who had helped him move it. Kevin's father sold as much of his portion as he dared, fearing that the English would suspect him if he brought in a full wagonload of grain when he had always raised potatoes in the past.

The family saved enough to use as seed for the next spring, and now Ma and Brigid were grinding the remain-ing wheat into flour. They used a simple hand mill made of

two flat stones. The top stone had a hole in the center
through which a stick was held as an axle, and around
which they poured the grain. There was a knob on one
side of the top stone which was used to turn it. Both stones
were placed on a tablecloth spread out on the ground to

catch the coarse flour as it slowly worked its way out from
between the two stones. It took Ma and Brigid a whole day
to grind enough flour for a batch of bread loaves—and
their hands were rubbed raw from it. Still, in Kevin's memory, it was a great treat. They rarely had bread more than
once or twice a year.

That first loaf was so delicious, cut in thick slices and
covered with fresh butter, that the family had eaten it all up
within five minutes of its emergence from the fireplace. Ma
had cooked it in her heaviest black iron pot, putting burning pieces of peat all around the sides and on the lid. Kevin
had never tasted anything so good. After that, Da and
Tom and Kevin had taken turns at grinding flour so they
could have this treat more often. It seemed to Kevin that
they had done nothing but grind flour and eat hot bread
for a whole week. This November had turned out better

than most Christmases, and Christmas was still to come. In fact, tomorrow was the first day of Advent, December first. Ma had promised to make them some sweet breads for Christmas if Da could afford to buy her a bit of sugar. Sugar! Now that was something Kevin rarely tasted. This Christmas was truly going to live up to the old Gaelic name, *oidhche na ceapairi*, the "night of cakes."

Kevin was very excited today, for there was to be a party tonight at the Donohues' house. Everyone they knew would be there—the Donohues of course, Kevin's friends Owen Morgan, Sean and Donal with their families from the village, the O'Reillys, the O'Mallorys, the Hennesseys, Father O'Flaherty, and several others. It would be a grand *ceili* since Mr. Donohue would not be giving another one on this side of the Atlantic. Kevin had never been to such an affair, since during his lifetime there had been little to celebrate in Ireland. Sometimes a fiddler would strike up some dancing, but little else. Tonight there was going to be a feast—and a real band. Even Ma and Da said that the last such *ceili* that either of them remembered had been before the '98 rebellion.

It was about three in the afternoon when they started the walk across the fields. The sun was already into the lower quarter of the sky, which meant that they would arrive just before twilight. Ma wanted to be there in time to help Rose and Mrs. Donohue set things up. Cathleen and Brigid ran from side to side looking for an occasional wild flower which had survived this late in the year. After a while, though, Tom was carrying Cathleen on his shoulders. When they reached the boreen leading to the Donohues' house, the shadows from the high stone walls felt suddenly chilly, but they kept to one side of the lane anyway. Timothy Donohue's accident had been near this spot, and they crossed themselves when Father reminded them of it. At last they came up out of the lane at the gate to Mr. Donohue's farm. The path leading to the house and barn was stoney, and almost as wide as the lane itself.

"Who was it laid down these stones, Da?" asked Kevin. It seemed that he was always noticing things these days that he had never taken notice of before, as if he were trying to memorize everything around him.

" 'Tis said it was none but your own Saint Kevin," said Father, "but no one knows for sure. This stone path leads on past Donohue's place off towards Ballygarrett, but I never walked it to its own end. Saint Kevin's shrine, and the selfsame church he built with his own hands are off north near Glendalough. That's forty miles or so. I'd not be the one to be denying that he did make this path, though what it was for there's no one could say."

Kevin looked down at the rounded stones that made up the path with a new appreciation. He felt that it must have been a very special road.

"Perhaps I'll be making one like it in Texas, to remind us of the Saint. I'll call it Saint Kevin's lane."

"It's a wild land we're going to, to be sure," said Tom, "with no roads at all but only tracks and trails, and much in need of civilizing. It's other things we'll be doing before we get down to building roads."

But Kevin had already decided that if Ma and Da and the family had to come to Texas in the future, there would be a stone path like this one for them to walk on. The sky had grown blue-green with the beginning of twilight, and cast its soft color on the land. Twilight in Ireland lasted well over an hour, and was the most pleasant time of the day. The sun was still holding a red sheen on the horizon, a delight to sailors, and the evening had not yet grown over-ly cold. Soon they saw several people coming out to meet them. Kevin ran to greet his friend Brian Ruadh O'Mallory, Jr. The "Ruadh" was because of his bright red hair. He was a freckle-faced boy Kevin's age, and as ornery as his father.

"Kevin," he shouted, "have you heard the news? We're to be going to Texas with you!"

"No," said Kevin, "are you really?"

"It's all settled," said Brian, "Father told my Ma that he couldn't bear to have her separated from her sister, that's Mrs. Donohue. So he said that we'd be going to Texas on the same boat. Da said that he'd been thinking about it for years and years and saving up the fare, but Ma thinks he's been selling poteen lately."

"Has he now?" said Kevin's father, just coming up to the two boys. "Well, I dare say when you get to Texas, you'll be needing a man with distilling skills—if only for medicinal purposes."

Laughing, the two boys ran up the path to the house while the rest of the family strolled behind. Sean and Donal were already there, and soon they had a short-handed game of hurly going. Mr. Donohue had a fine set of hurly sticks he had made long ago as a birthday present for his son, and all the boys in the area coveted them.

Tom and Father watched the boys get the game start-ed. Tom said, "If Mr. O'Mallory's been at distilling poteen, then it's sure to be better than your average poison whisky. I've heard him tell how, when he was younger, he used to work in a regular distillery up north."

"Aye, that's true enough," said Father, "but don't you go drinking too much of it till you see how it takes with other folks. A man can't be watching a pot still hidden away in a cave somewhere all the time, so he can't be sure what the product is going to be like. There's some poteen's driven men mad. Still," he said with a smile, "I can't think Brian would bring anything not worth tasting to a party the likes of this one at his own brother-in-law's house."

Inside, Ma and Brigid and Cathleen had joined the other women in laying out the tables with fresh breads and platters of roast pig and beef, rare treats indeed. From one of the outbuildings came a fine smokey, meaty smell. Mr. Donohue had just finished curing a quantity of beef into a tough salted jerky they could take on the ship with them. When they heard this, Tom and Kevin agreed that the food, at least, would be better on the voyage than their normal fare at home. Mr. Donohue had killed the last of his cattle to make the jerky. He had sold all of his pigs before the redcoats had come for his grain, lest they take the stock as well. As it turned out, the soldiers did take most of his sheep. One pig had been hidden in their turf loft, saved especially for this party.

Soon there were nearly forty people in and around the house, *colloughing* with each other in the pleasant twilight. The length and pleasantness of this time of day, when it seemed that all Ireland stopped to gossip and relax, was largely responsible for the way in which news, stories, history, poetry, and songs were passed from person to person and from generation to generation. This evening was no exception, but the talk was of one thing only—Texas. Tonight there were no stories of leprechauns or banshees, no tales of ancient or modern heroes, tonight it was all turned toward the new lands so far across the western seas. Kevin found that, thanks to all the family's talk recently, and to his inquisitive probing of the school-master, he seemed to know as much about Texas as anyone there. Soon he was answering questions like a well-travelled poet.

As the curlews called, the larks twittered, and the sky's greenish light deepened into a velvety blue-black, Kevin talked on and on about how Texas must be the very place for the Irish. It was so green in the south along the coast, and hadn't the Spanish been enemies of England for time out of mind? To say nothing of the United States having an Irishman for president at this very minute! Kevin's chatter was only broken by the sound of Father O'Flaherty calling them in for supper. He was tapping one of Mrs. Donohue's crystal glasses with a spoon, making a clear belling sound that carried across the yard and seemed to go on past them into the hills. Soon everyone was crowding to get a place at the three long tables. Lanterns, open candles, and rush lights were everywhere. Kevin had never seen it so bright this late at night.

Father O'Flaherty said the grace, in which he thanked God for letting him see so much food, for once in his life, all in one place and so generously given to "these good folk of this destitute isle. Not forsaken, Lord, for we remember well your promises to our patron, Saint Patrick, but desti-tute with the miseries of a conquered land." The priest finished by calling down the blessings of Christ and more Saints than Kevin had even heard of on the Donohues and on all who journeyed with them to that "far land sought by the good Saint Brendan."

That was new to Kevin. His second name was Brendan. He would have to get the priest to tell him more about the voyages of Saint Brendan. But now everyone's attention was on the food before them. Kevin was almost ashamed of how much he was eating, except that everyone else seemed to be enjoying it as much as he was. Meat —real roast beef and pork; Kevin could hardly believe it. Very few of the people at the party had ever eaten their fill of such a luxury. At home, a small bit of meat was made to go as far as it could. That usually meant boiling it into a broth and then using it in stew. The only meat they had regularly was fish, or scallops. Kevin had no idea that Mr. Donohue was so rich, and he said as much to Tom.

"Aye, he's that rich by our standards, Kevin. But just think of his position. Another year and the English would sure have taxed him off what remains of his family lands and out of this very house. He hasn't a son to inherit it, so the land would go to the Crown rather than to Mrs. Donohue or Rose. That's the law. If he wasn't going to Texas, I don't doubt but what he'd be taking his chances with the landlords just like us in a couple of years."

"Nah, it wouldn't be as bad as that, Tom," said Father. "But it's bad manners and bad luck to be talking of such things while you're eating of Mr. Donohue's food and at his own table." Just then, Mr. Donohue got up and prepared to give a speech.

"Father," he said nodding to the priest, "and friends,

there's a great deal of news to be telling, and since most of it concerns myself, I'm thinking it's best for me to be doing the telling of it. Everyone here knows, of course, that I'm moving my family across the waters to Texas. We don't know just when the ship will be leaving yet, but it's sure that we won't be seeing many of you again in this life. So I'd like to be saying how much we love you all, and how much we wish that Ireland was in such a state that we could stay here among such good friends and die and be buried alongside our fathers and their fathers in these green hills. But," he said, wiping his eyes dry, "that's a thing past wishing. I hear that young Kevin Dolan here is dreaming he'll be bringing back an army of Americans to free Eire. That's as it may be, and a noble notion. For me, I think it's best that we take a bit of Ireland to this new country and be thinking of it not as an exile soon to be ended, but as a new Ireland. Sure, in time, we'll have some Gaelic saints walking that new land—even if it's Spanish or even English that they'll be speaking."

At that everyone laughed, and someone shouted, "Raise a revolution and name the land *Nua Eire*. Then we'll be coming over in droves even if we have to be sailing there in *curraghs* like Saint Brendan."

"Well, Tom Hennessey," said Mr. Donohue, identifying the speaker, "I'd like to be seeing the likes of you, a potato farmer all your born days, handling a *curragh* on the deep seas, but anything can happen. But what I mainly have to be telling you is this, that I have sold my land." Raising his hands to quiet the sudden exclamations and whispering, he said, "It's gone to a Mr. Jonathon Moran of

Dublin, and I won't stint telling you that he got it for less than it's worth. But he seems a fair man. Like myself, he's a Catholic even if he puts up a braw front to the English that he's a high kirk Protestant. I made him swear by all the saints, Jesus and Mary, on his own family Bible that he won't be gouging you like most landlords these days, and told him that if he was after breaking his word on that, he'd be a man forsworn and not worth a hoot or a hoolee to the folks around here. I don't know if he's to be as good as his word, but at least you'll have that to curse him with.

"The other thing I wanted to tell you was who all would be going to Texas on our ship. My sister-in-law's family, the O'Mallorys, will be with us, and I'm taking Tom and Kevin Dolan. The Dolan boys will be working for me for the space of a year, and then they'll be getting their own land. There'll also be a good many folk from Wexford and Ballygarrett, and one for sure will be Pegeen O'Grady, the tavern mistress of the Vinegar Hill in Enniscorthy. Now, let's get on with the dancing and the music before Advent comes and the Christmas fast begins."

Suddenly everyone was in motion, cleaning up the food, pushing the tables back to the edge of the room, rearranging the candles and lanterns. The musicians gathered at the front of the room. The drummer was dipping his fingers in a cup of water and flicking the water on the inside of his *bodhron*'s sheepskin head. Then he tested the sound of the drum with a short thick drumstick. He used both ends of the stick, tapping back and forth, to create a low rolling sound. The fiddler was tuning to the tin whistle, as was a man playing a wooden flute.

The drummer broke into a rhythm that immediately set everyone's feet to tapping. Kevin knew the tune at once. It was by Blind Raftery, a double jig by the name of "Maire ni Eidhin." Everyone knew that Raftery had written the words for the tune for the fairest colleen ever to walk the hills of Eire. It was a fiddle tune, but soon the tin whistle and flute were trading off on the melody, for the sake of keeping the dance going. Tom and Mary and several others were jigging furiously, and didn't even break step when the fiddler began to play a second jig, "Gillan's Apples," in the middle of one of the repetitions of the Raftery tune. Soon the whistle and flute followed the new tune, and yet another jig followed. After about twenty minutes of constant music, the band stopped for a round of poteen. While the dancers rested, the flute played a slow air, "An Mhaighdean Mhara," about a mermaid who married a mortal. Tom and Mary sat down next to Kevin.

"What a night this has been," said Tom.

"That's some fine jigging you two were at," said Kevin. "I thought you'd dance your way through the floor. I didn't know you had it in you at all."

"Kevin," said Mary, "I've never known an Irish lad who had none of the jig in his feet. Wouldn't you like to be joining me next round?"

Kevin was embarrassed, but Tom came to his aid. "Mary, the boy would never be living it down before his friends," he said. "You know a boy his age never dances with an older lass like yourself."

"But he'll be leaving Eire and his friends in such a short while. It couldn't hurt at all to be doing at least one dance on the soil of Eire before he has to dance with some

Spanish maid off in America where he won't be knowing the steps or the music at all. Come on, Kevin, they're start-ing again."

"Let him be," said Tom, "you'll embarrass the lad."

But again that sense of looking closely at things he had never noticed before had come over Kevin. Like the stones in the path outside, dancing the old jigs and reels to the music he loved—dancing them with a girl, that is—was something Kevin had never really thought about. Until a few minutes ago, he had thought it quite funny to see his brother stepping so lightly and whirling like a top, but now it seemed the only thing to be doing. Besides, he couldn't bear Tom's talking about him as if he were only a child.

"I'll do it, by Pat," he said, and took Mary's out-stretched hand. To Tom he said, "It's old enough I am to go to Texas and it's old enough I am to be dancing with your colleen." Mary laughed, but Tom gave him a look it would be hard to forget.

The band was just finishing up an air called "The White Cockade." It had been played by the Irish pipers at the Battle of Fontenoy in 1745 when the pipers had turned the tide of battle in favor of the French over the English. Remembering that stirred Kevin's blood. The next one was a reel, a fast one; Kevin did not know its name.

Before he realized what was happening, Kevin was dancing, flinging his legs high and angular, face to face with Mary, arms stiff at his side and whirling by himself, jump-ing to the music and landing on his toes. His toes! Kevin suddenly realized that he must be the only barefoot dancer on the floor. Although he tried to stop it, he began to feel steamy around his neck as the red blush came to his face.

He would never live this down, even in America. Surely
Brian Ruadh would remind him of it to the end of his days.
How could he have been so stupidly sentimental? Tom's
words bit deeply now—"a boy his age never dances with
an older lass." He had walked into this one for sure, and it
would give Tom another reason to think of him as just
a silly lad.

Mary broke in on his thoughts when she leaned close
and said, "Kevin, what's wrong at all? Surely we can't have
winded a lad like you."

"Yes, a lad," he thought. Kevin looked down, but kept
on dancing. "It's barefooted I am," he said at their next
close pass.

"Oh, is that it?" asked Mary, looking genuinely re-
lieved. With a motion so fluid it looked surely to be a part
of the dance, Mary bent down twice and held up her
ribbon-trimmed dancing shoes. She caught Tom's eye and
pitched the shoes into his lap.

"I can't keep up with your brother so encumbered,"
she laughed.

Suddenly Kevin felt cooler, if still rather foolish. Dancing was all right, he decided—at least dancing with Mary
O'Reilly. He had begun, at last, to see a bit of what Tom
saw in her.

"Sure I won't mind having Mary for a sister-in-law,"
he told Tom later, when the dancing was over and the
musicians were lullabying the children. "She was fine at
the hurly, and she's finer at the dancing."

Tom, on the other hand, saw little humorous about it.
"I told you you were too young to be dancing with Mary—
coming lame to a *ceili* without a brogan on your foot at all,
not even a pair of my old gear. You're nothing but an em-
barrassment sometimes, Kevin Dolan. I won't have my
wife that's to be taking off her shoes in public again for
you."

That really upset Kevin. Mary had been very kind
under the circumstances. "Remember your words, big
brother," said Kevin. "You told her not to be dancing with
the likes of me, not the other way around. Besides, I
wouldn't want to be wearing any of your old brogans."

"If that's the way of it, little brother," said Tom, "then
you'd better be taking off your pants as well, for there's not
a stitch of cloth on you that I haven't worn before."

It was true, as Kevin well knew. But before, it had been something to be proud of; before, whenever he had gotten one of Tom's old shirts, it had made him feel older for a few days. Now, there seemed something vaguely shameful about it all. Mary was none too pleased with Tom for talking to Kevin so, and she was busy whispering fiercely into Tom's ear when Da and Ma came to the table.

"First lover's spat, I'll warrant," said Father affably. "What is it Tom, has she told you at last that her womanly skills don't run to cooking buffalo and shooting Indians?"

"Now Da," said their Mother, "I don't recall that you cared whether I could boil a potato at all when you were courting me."

At that, they all laughed. Brigid and Cathleen were already asleep in a corner of the room near the fire. Kevin was so full of good food, and so tired from the dancing and excitement that he was ready to fall down himself. Many people had already left to walk home if they lived close enough, but several of the neighbors were going to stay the night. All around them, people were spreading out blankets on the floor. Kevin had just begun to lie down when they heard a boy shouting outside. Owen Morgan, a boy Brigid's age, came panting into the room.

"Soldiers," he gasped. "Redcoats. They ran down my father in the lane near the village. I got away over the hill. Da said to tell you they're coming here." With that he turned back to the door.

"Where is it you're going to now, Owen?" asked Kevin's father, stopping Owen at the door.

"I think they killed my father. I've got to get back to my Ma."

"You stay here and we'll go tend to her," said Mr. Hennessey. "Father O'Flaherty, can you come with me?"

"Sure man, I'm right behind you," said the priest. "The protection of Jesus, Mary, and Joseph be on you all this night," he called out, making a wild cross in the air. Then they were gone into the dark.

"Now, Owen," said Mr. Dolan, "are you hurt at all? And did you hear the soldiers say what they were about?"

"No, sir, I'm not hurt. I think they're coming just to be breaking up the party but they're in a dark mood. They didn't even stop over my Da. The last thing he said was to warn you, so I ran here directly over the hill. They can't be far behind even with them staying to the road."

"You've done well, Owen Morgan," said Mr. Donohue, "but now drink this." He handed him a cup of tea spiked with poteen, for it was clear that the boy was very agitated by all that had happened.

Taking the cup, he said, "I think my Da's dead. I could hear my Ma keening before I was gone half a mile."

Mr. Dononue held him close for a moment, then turned to the crowd and said in a loud voice, "You women, put out the lights and get the children into the fields, and take Owen with you. Quick now. Mr. Dolan, see what you can do about emptying what poteen is still about and pitch the jugs in the gulley out back. Mrs. Donohue, you'd better get your best things clear of the house."

There was a great bustling to clear away any evidence of the party. Although there was no official curfew these days, the English were always upset when there was a gathering of Irishmen of any size at all. Tom picked up Brigid, still asleep, and Kevin picked up Cathleen. They ran with Ma far out of the house, but close enough that they could still hear and see what went on. They plopped the frightened, sleepy girls on the ground and ran back to help the others. The house was dark now, but in the moonlight you could see men running this way and that. And you could hear a troop of horses coming up the stone path.

"Thanks be to Saint Kevin for that path of his," said Father as he pushed the boys back up the hill to where they had left the girls and Ma. Each had a bundle or a box which Mrs. Donohue had all but thrown into their arms from the door. On the hill, Owen and the O'Mallorys had joined the Dolans. Below, they could hear the redcoats come to a halt in front of the house. It had been less than five minutes since Owen had run through the door. Some of the soldiers were carrying torches. Creeping back down the hill a bit, they could hear Mr. Donohue asking the soldiers what it was they would be wanting at such an hour.

It was the English Major that Tom had unsaddled who was leading the troop. He seemed a bit drunk to Kevin, but Father said later that sometimes men were that way when they held the power of life and death over another man. The rest of the troop was restless, as if they knew that they were surrounded by the Irish. The Major was speaking.

"We were told by a Mr. Morgan," he said with a smirk, "that you were holding a meeting out here—a revolutionary meeting perhaps."

"That's a lie," Owen said out loud, and he started to scramble up.

Kevin tackled him, telling him to be quiet. "We know it's a lie, Owen," he said, "Who among *us* here would be believing a thing that snake down there was saying?"

"They know who it was they trampled in the road," said Tom.

"Why, no," Mr. Donohue was saying to the Major, as polite as could be, "we were only after having a bit of an Advent *ceili*. Everybody's gone on home now. Why don't you go on, too; it's late it is and getting cold."

"Well, we cannot let a report like that go without an investigation," said the Major, nudging his horse toward Mr. Donohue. "Now stand aside. Sergeant," he roared out. "Search the house and seize anything that might be evidence."

Several redcoats dismounted and approached the doorway carrying torches and large canvas bags. But Mr. Donohue did not move from his door.

"Stand aside, I said," shouted the Major.

"Before you go entering this house with no good cause, I should warn you that it's not my own house any more. I'm just after selling it to Mr. Jonathon Moran of Dublin, a name you might know."

"Is that so? Do you have that deed of sale about your person or is this more of your paddywhackery? I'd like to see it," he said with another grunting laugh.

Mr. Donohue reached inside his coat for his wallet. At that, one of the soldiers fired a pistol which struck the door just an inch above Mr. Donohue's shoulder. He didn't flinch, but handed the papers up to the Major.

"It's a good thing your friend with the pistol is such a bad shot. I assume it is a crime, even in England, to be killing an unarmed man on his own doorstep."

The Major snorted and studied the deed of sale by torchlight. Looking up, he said, "Patrick Eamonn Donohue, this deed is dated over five days ago. Why are you still here?"

"If you'll look in the third paragraph, you'll see that Mr. Moran won't be taking possession until the new year."

"Hold that torch closer, soldier," the Major said to the

man mounted beside him. He made a great show of examining the document, holding the paper so close to the torch that the paper actually began to smoulder.

"Do you see anything to that effect?" he asked the man holding the torch.

"No sir!" the man replied crisply without bothering to look at the paper.

"In my opinion, Donohue, you're trespassing on Mr. Moran's property, and possibly you sold it to finance treasonous activities. Sergeant!" he shouted again. "Search the house."

The soldiers pushed Mr. Donohue roughly aside and entered the house. They could be heard, even up on the hill, shouting and throwing things around. You could hear chairs being broken and crockery being smashed. Kevin and Owen were all for attacking them while they were so distracted, but Father pointed out that they had no weapons—not even rakes or pitchforks—and that a troop of armed soldiers was not to be overcome by throwing stones. Mr. Donohue and the Major stood squared off in front of the house. The Dolans crept down the hill so they could hear over the noise the soldiers were making inside. Kevin picked up two round stones as they crawled, just to be safe.

"We know the part you played in the '98 rebellion," the Major was saying, "and by rights you should have been hanged then. Still, I can't hang a man for crimes thirty years old, though I ought to. But this trespassing, I'm afraid you'll have to be off this land—tonight." He was laughing an evil laugh when the Sergeant returned.

"Nothing, sir," the Sergeant said. "It looks like the place has been pretty well cleaned out except for the furniture and some dishes."

"Did you examine the furniture and the dishes thoroughly, Sergeant?"

"Yes sir," he replied, "we even pulled up some floorboards."

"Well done," said the Major. "All right, Donohue, you heard what I said. You're trespassing on the land of Mr. Jonathon Moran, and I want you out of here by morning. I'll be back to set a guard on this place tomorrow until Mr. Moran comes to take possession of it."

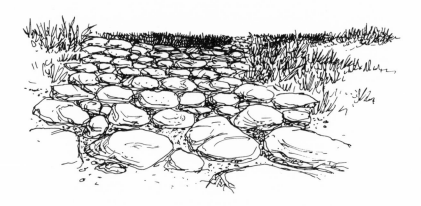

*Chapter 4*

# A Long Winter Night

The farewells that night were more sorrowful than anyone had expected. When the sound of the soldiers' horses cantering down the stone path had disappeared into the soft dust of the boreen, and Kevin, Owen, and Brian Ruadh had flung many stones after them, the families began to come down from the hills around the house. There were still some twenty people about. The night was turning very cold, and almost everyone was coughing and sneezing from lying on the ground so long. They built up the fire in the house—this time with some of the broken furniture—and gathered around it to get warm and dry again.

Some of the men were in favor of going into the village and burning out the redcoats then and there, but Mr. Donohue calmed them into more peaceful endeavors. Mrs. Donohue had packed many of her best things before the party, and these boxes and bags had been carried out of the house just before the soldiers' arrival. It turned out that the box which Kevin had carried up the hill contained teacups and glasses. Kevin told Tom that he was glad he had not known what was in the box, or he would surely have dropped it. Tom agreed. Now they were busy packing everything the Donohues wanted to take with them onto their one cart.

It was illegal, and certainly unfair, for the redcoats to make the Donohues move in the middle of the night. But Mr. Donohue said that he was so tired of dealing with English injustices that he would rather just get away. The English hated him for holding on to his land so long, and there was no telling what else they might try to do to him before he could get safely off to America. It was the same for almost everyone. After a while, what was once terrifying became part of daily life.

Some of the men were set to packing the jerky into two large barrels, while others gathered Mr. Donohue's tools and farming equipment from the sheds and fields. It was cold work. Everyone had come dressed in their best

clothes and were not prepared to be doing such heavy work in the middle of a cold night. From a distance, the Donohue farm must have looked a haunted place, with the torches moving back and forth across the yard and the fields. At last, everything that was going to Texas had been packed into, or on top of, or hung from the sides of, the cart.

"We're surely gypsies now, Ma," said Mr. Donohue to his wife.

"Aye, but at least we have the chance of getting off to the new world. The way things have been going from bad to worse, we could have been stranded like tinkers for sure on the boreens of Eire until we died of old age by a campfire in the hills of Connemara. There's worse off than us for sure."

For all her brave front, everyone could see that Mrs. Donohue hated to leave this place that had been her home for so long. Rose was worse. She had not stopped weeping since the soldiers had first come. She had been quite

hysterical when her father had been shot at by the English soldier. "No more," she wailed out, "I'll not be taking any more hardship from the likes of those blaggarts and ruffians," and then she broke into her keening and sobbing again. Mr. Donohue let her cry against his shoulder for a long time. With the work done, the men sat shivering around the fireplace once more while their women rubbed their backs and shoulders, and buffed the cold out of their hands and feet. Kevin had never been so tired in all his life, and was barely able to keep his eyes open as Cathleen —wide awake after her nap earlier in the evening—rubbed his feet with her rough red wool cloak.

"Well, there's one more job to be done this night before the redcoats come back," said Mr. Donohue. Everyone groaned, but began to get up again. "No, no," he said, "sit back down. It's only to be asking you to divide up what's left of this furniture among yourselves. Sure I was going to play the squire and drive around the countryside giving it away in a grand style, but now it must be gone before morning. Sure I couldn't abide the thought of that fat Major resting his backside in my favorite chair."

Everyone laughed at that and began to look around to see what was left. There were the three large tables and some smaller ones, a few unbroken chairs, two bedsteads, and other things which would cost too much to ship to Texas. They were busy dividing these things up when Mr. Hennessey returned.

"*Go mbeannuighe Dia annso*—God bless all here. Where's Owen?" he said.

Completely exhausted with his desperate run across the hills earlier that night, and with the rest of the night's excitement and hard labor (and numbed with the poteen which Rose had been putting in his tea), Owen had collapsed in a heap by the fire.

"Is it bad at all?" asked Mr. Dolan.

"Aye, and worse, Stephen. The redcoats have done for the whole family."

"What? How did it happen? Mrs. Morgan too?" came from everyone.

Mr. Hennessey sat down. "It was like this," he said slowly. "The Father and myself found Mrs. Morgan keening over the body of her husband in the middle of the road just outside the village. He was all trampled, like the whole troop had passed over him. I'm surprised indeed that he lived long enough to send Owen to warn us. But there she was, wailing out curses on the English like a banshee on *Samain* night. Father gave him the last rites there in the road, and then we moved his body to their cottage. It was no more than five minutes' walk—that close they were to their own door. We were trying to get her comforted with prayers and then with whiskey and then with prayers again. Then she heard the soldiers coming down the lane again, and up she flies, crying that she'd cast a curse on them would never wash off even if they all were baptised by the Pope and bathed in holy water nine times a day. We tried to keep her down, but she threw us off—that strong willed she was. Up she jumps and runs out into the road, right in front of the troop, screaming out a Gaelic curse it would freeze your bones to hear, calling down calamities from boils to the black death on them and their sons and their cattle and on anything they ever owned or loved or ever would. And then herself went down under the horses just like Mr. Morgan had. Then Father had to give her the rites too, and I came on back here. It's been a terrible night for the Irish in these parts."

"I'm thinking it will be a terrible life for those redcoats. God bring 'em an ill wind, for a widow's curses are not to be ignored, and she being murdered in their uttering. It's glad I am I wasn't there to be hearing such a thing." It was Mrs. Dolan speaking. "But sure, what's to be done with Owen now he's a poor orphan lad?"

Rose spoke up now. She had recovered from her hysterical crying, though her voice still cracked. Kevin thought that she sounded different, somehow stronger. "Don't be calling him poor nor an orphan, for he'll be going away from this cursed land with us. I never wanted a husband nor a child, nor a nunnery as you might wonder, but I'm saying now I have a child, and Owen Morgan is himself."

Mrs. Donohue turned to her husband and said, "It's only fitting that we take the child, Patrick, since it was himself that brought the warning that saved us this night. What if the redcoats had come in sudden-like and found you with an illegal jug in your hand? And look at the way they smashed up what little was in here. There's not a plate in the wash tubs that didn't catch a rifle butt, and what if they'd taken your money box as 'evidence' . . ."

"I've no qualms at all about taking young Owen with us, but don't you think you had better be asking him whether he'd like our Rose as his new mother? He might have other ideas. But right now he's getting the sleep he needs and deserves. Leave him be until we can talk it over in the light of day. Mr. Dolan, would you be minding it at all if we drove over to your place to spend a day and a night? It's too far to go on to Margaret's sister's place tonight."

"Sure, 'twould be our pleasure, but I'm thinking we'd best be getting on with it before the sun comes up and brings the Major's guard with it."

With that, they loaded Owen, still limp with exhaustion and poteen, up onto the driver's bench with Mr. Donohue. He whipped up the team and began to move the creaking wagon down the stone path for the last time in his life. The remaining neighbors began to carry the furniture they had been given as far out into the fields as they could before first light. After the treatment Mr. Donohue had received at the hands of the redcoats, there was no telling what the soldiers would do if they caught a man hauling the furniture out of the place. Probably shoot him as a looter. When dawn finally came, sudden and bright, the house which last night had been the scene of such merriment was empty of all but the wind, swinging the open door back and forth.

# Part Two

*Chapter 5*

# The *Prudence* Sets Sail

Liverpool was terrible.

It was worse than any description Kevin had ever heard of it, and he had never heard anything good. Here it was Christmas Day, and still the dock hands and some of the sailors were hard at work loading their ship. "When a ship's to sail, it has to be loaded," was the explanation he had gotten from Nat MacBride, the American First Mate. Kevin had to admit that today was much quieter than those previous. There were only two or three ships where Kevin could tell that work was going on, but still, it seemed to Kevin that it must be a very great sin for anyone to carry on as if this were any other day of the year.

Kevin leaned over the gunwale and watched the stevedores swinging their lethal-looking cargo hooks and toting great lengths of heavy rope. Some of the ropes ran through so many pulleys that Kevin had a hard time tracing which rope was which. There seemed to be something dangerous and snake-like about the rope's slow uncurling from the huge coils on the dock, but even so it reminded him of the stone cross back home with its swirling inter-laced designs.

It was difficult for Kevin to put the events of the last month into any sort of order. It seemed as if a whirlwind had picked him up and dropped him here, on the bow of a rather small ship in a strange fog-shrouded city of English-men. After the pre-dawn flight from the Donohue farm, they had gotten word that the first of Mr. Power's ships would be sailing from Liverpool on the day after Christ-mas. At almost the same time, they had heard that the English soldiers were hunting for Mr. Donohue. Since, as Ma had put it, it was "hardly likely that the Major only wants to be bidding Mr. Donohue a fair wind to his back", it had been decided that they would go down to Wexford and sail for Liverpool on the first ship available.

The port of Wexford was much smaller than Liver-pool, and it seemed to Kevin that it had been a happier place as well. Bright in the December sunshine, the docks had been filled with well-wishers and stevedores singing old Gaelic songs of the sea in time to their work. Ma and Da and Brigid and Cathleen had all been there, as well as Michael's family and Mary O'Reilly and a number of others from their parish. Kevin could hear them still, shouting from the dock for Tom to take care of Kevin and for Kevin to take care of Tom—that had been from Mary. Tom had been beside him then, waving with one arm and hugging Kevin with the other while the ship had put on sail and nudged out into the Irish Sea. The last thing they heard from the shore was the great voice of Tom Hennessey calling out, "Go with the wind, Kevin Dolan . . . and Tom

. . . and Patrick Eamonn . . . with the wind at all your backs . . ."

Soon Ireland was nothing but a green line, looking like a stack of upside-down saucers as the low hills mounted up against the horizon. It was then, as Eire slipped away behind them, that the weeping began. If they had not done so before, the passengers had to face the fact then that few of them would ever see those green shores again. But they could never have guessed just how few that number would be. Kevin tried hard to keep in mind that he, for one, would return one day, but all the dreams he had for future glories seemed pale in comparison to the grief of this parting.

"It's like watching someone you loved die too young," Tom said to him, and hugged him tighter, both of their faces wet with the streaming tears.

But here in the Liverpool fog there was no singing. It was strangely absent, to Kevin's mind, since it was Christmas Day. The stevedores below Kevin cursed at the cold, and at the slippery gangway, even at the money they would make that day. It seemed like everyone was miserable in Liverpool.

Yesterday the quay had been lined with hordes of emigrants—Irish, Scot, Welsh, and even English. All were wretchedly poor, stinking of the rat-infested and over-priced rooms that swelled to bursting along most of the streets in this dank city on the Mersey River. Kevin had heard of "merry old England," but he could not imagine a more dreary place. The Mersey was shrouded in a dense haze which had not lifted since their arrival. All the smells of the dirty town hung in the air, mixing with the ship smells of lye, tar, salt, and spar varnish. Kevin's nostrils burned with it all.

What Kevin wanted to smell was fresh hot bread, and he wanted to hear Brigid's taunts and the laughter of Michael's new baby. If he and Tom had not had to rush off to catch this ship, the family would have been walking back from Mass just about now. After that there would have been little sweet breads and soda bread rolls for them, fresh and dripping with butter, and a fresh pot of tea. And singing. There would have been lots of singing and all the other little customs and ceremonies that Kevin so loved about Christmas.

First, at sunset on Christmas Eve, they would set out the Christmas candle. That could be done only by someone in the family named Mary. Ma had always done it in the past, as her full name was Mary Brigid O'Connel Dolan, but this year little Cathleen would get to do it for the first time since her middle name was Mary. Cathleen had been looking forward to lighting the Christmas candle for months. It would be the first time she had ever been allowed to stay up so late and Da—Kevin could imagine this so well—Da would dance her around the cottage on his shoulders. Kevin hoped they had been just a little happy last night, even with Tom and himself gone away. He crossed himself and prayed that his family would take some joy in the day. But he knew that his mother was crying.

At that moment, the English were more hateful to Kevin than perhaps ever before, and he spat over the gunwale in distaste. Even the Christmas traditions were bound up with their oppression. The Christmas candle was a reminder of the days when the English had hunted down Catholic priests like so many foxes or coneys. Every Catholic family wanted to hear Mass on Christmas night, so they put a candle in their window to let any priest who might be passing know that their house was a safe haven. To the English it was explained as a quaint custom—a light for Mary and Joseph, should they come seeking shelter in the night. Every Christmas sermon, the priest would draw the parallel—Mary bearing Jesus, the priest bearing the sacrament—so that Kevin had grown comfortable with both explanations. But even though he loved the custom because it had always been a part of his family's Christmas, Kevin could not keep himself from wishing that he could take something of Ireland with him that had not been besmirched by the English. The last straw was that they had taken this Christmas away from him altogether. The wind cut through the mist and made Kevin shiver with the cold. He turned and was about to walk back to the miserable rooms where his group had been staying for over a week when he heard his name called.

Rose Donohue was coming over the gangway as quick as she could, dodging the stevedores and their heavy loads, holding up her skirts with one hand and balancing her wiry frame by waving the other hand wildly about. Out of breath, she called to Kevin again.

"Kevin, Kevin lad, have you seen Owen at all? He's been gone from our rooms the length of this day since before we were up. I cannot find a trace of him and was thinking surely he might be here with you on the boat. Oh, the wee thing's been stolen away, I know. Mrs. O'Grady was just saying that there's bound to be gypsies or white slavers or somesuch in a town such as this . . ."

Kevin was trying, unsuccessfully, to calm Rose and get some more information out of her when Mr. MacBride strode up.

"Nat MacBride, ma'am, First Mate to the *Prudence*," he said introducing himself. "Now what's all this blathering about? Your lad's missing, you say?"

"It's my wee boy; he's about ten with dark hair all in the fairest curls. He's been gone since before we got up and I know he's fallen into the Mersey because of your filthy English fog, or else he's been stolen away, or . . ."

"Pardon, but it's not my fog, ma'am. I'm an American. But he's a dark headed lad, you say, about so tall?" He held his hand about shoulder high to Kevin, at which Rose nodded her head vigorously. Then Mr. MacBride cupped his hands and shouted with a very loud sort of hallooing voice, "Owen!"

Both Kevin and Rose were surprised to hear that the First Mate knew who they were talking about, much less knew his name, and they followed the tall American's gaze into the mist-hidden spider web of rigging above them.

"Mr. Morgan," came the shout again, ever so much like he was ordering one of his seamen, "fo'c'sle immediately."

From high above them, Owen's voice floated down, "Aye aye, sir. Coming." Turning to the flustered Rose, Mr. MacBride said, "He's a very bright lad you've got, Mrs. Morgan. Been after me since yesterday morning to tell him one thing or another about seafaring. He's a sailor born and no doubt of it, and I don't mind him tagging along behind me at all. But it would speed things up a bit for me if you could take him home for a spell."

"My name is Rose Donohue," began Rose, "You see, Owen is a poor orphan lad." And she began to explain about Owen's parents and how they were taking him to Texas now, and was just explaining how one of Owen's great-grandfathers had been a Welsh house servant to an English lord when Owen himself came rattling down the foremast shroud. Swinging off the ropes, he landed beside Rose, who at once stopped what she was saying to the First Mate and began to lecture Owen. Then she turned on the officer again and began to chide him for letting such a fragile boy go climbing about so high in the rigging that he would "no doubt be hanging himself or getting lost in the clouds so close to heaven."

"Hold, hold now, stow it a while, Miss Donohue," he said. "Owen here is no wee fragile thing. He's a good sturdy lad, and agile as a cat in the rigging. I'd say he has a good future in front of him on the sea, if you'll be letting him follow his instincts. But I must be getting back to my work or the Master'll see *me* swing from a yardarm. Good day, Miss Donohue; I'll see you boys again when we're under way."

All the way back to their lodgings, Owen could talk of nothing but the ship. That night, Kevin and Brian Ruadh sat up late listening to Owen explain all sorts of things about how ships really worked—about how there were some 300 separate ropes, each with its own name and its own function, about the parts of the ship, and where the guns would go if she were armed, and on and on.

When Kevin finally lay down, he was already dreaming of the day when Owen would pilot him back across the Atlantic, with an army. But what Kevin found oddly absent, and would miss more as their voyage went on, was Owen's fury at the English.

The morning after the Donohue's party, when they had first told Owen that both his parents had been killed, it was all they could do to keep him from running off to join some group of rebels. He was all tears and curses and rage. Even Kevin had tried to talk him out of running away, telling him that they would go to America and come back better soldiers, worth more to Ireland than mere boys. But somehow, overnight almost, Owen had changed. It reminded Kevin of how Tom seemed to forget everything else when he was thinking about Mary O'Reilly. "That must be it," thought Kevin as he rolled over on the stinking mattress. "Owen's fallen in love with the sea, like one of the fair folk in Mr. O'Mallory's stories."

The next morning, Mr. Donohue and Mr. O'Mallory had a hard time rousing the boys. It was very early, long before dawn, and the men had to shake them awake. But soon they were all on their feet and, after a cup of thin tea, trudging down the dark street toward the docks. Other folk of their ship joined them as they neared the Mersey, and their spirits began to rise despite the early hour and the cold wet wind blowing down the river. The boys felt a sense of high adventure about it and everyone was glad to be leaving Liverpool. Here, there were no farewells to be said, no loved ones left on the shore, no tears to be shed. Soon they were walking up the gangway of the *Prudence*.

Having stowed the last of their things away in the small spaces allotted them in the steerage compartment between decks, the passengers all came topside to watch their departure. The sailors kept them crowded together amidships, out of the way. With first light, the tide started to run, and the *Prudence* cast off. Even at that early hour, the passengers let out a cheer when they felt the ship's first movement. Once in mid-channel, they began to put on sail. In no time at all, Liverpool was receding into its mists and dank odors as the *Prudence* pushed out into the Irish Sea. The Catholic emigrants were busy saying their voyaging prayers to the Virgin Mother, to St. Christopher, and to their own name-saints. Kevin vowed again to St. Kevin that if he arrived safely in Texas, he would build a stone path there in memory of the Saint. He made no vows of returning though, because he could think of no Christian way of putting it in a prayer. Still, as the sun burned off the mists, and England sank below the horizon, Kevin did not think of much else but his eventual return.

Owen, on the other hand, seemed bent on forgetting all about Ireland and the English. He delighted in watching the sailors at their work, and was overjoyed to do any little errand that Mr. MacBride could think up for him. It was strange that this little Welsh/Irish boy who had rarely even seen the sea before leaving Wexford did not get in the way of the burly old salts whose business it was to guide their small ship to Texas. The sailors all seemed to take to him at once, as if they recognized something of themselves in him—something they certainly did not see in Kevin or Brian Ruadh. Whenever *they* asked one of the seamen a

question, the answer was short, and the men were generally impatient with the two boys who seemed always in
their way. Kevin was sure that if he were caught climbing
about in the rigging the way Owen did, some crusty old
sailor would chuck him over the stern. At last, weary of
being told to move here, go over there, and get out of the
way, Kevin and Brian Ruadh settled themselves in an out-
of-the-way corner where they could enjoy the scene
without being stepped on.

Almost everyone had brought along some cold food
for the first few meals, so there was no necessity of lighting
up any cooking fires. Kevin wished that someone would
light a fire somewhere, however, as it was getting colder
by the hour. The wind was no longer steady but shifted
this way and that, causing the sailors to be constantly
clambering about in the rigging to shift the sails. This
became so constant an activity that some of them re-
mained aloft, standing erect on a yardarm, holding on to a
mast or a stay line. They made it look so easy, thought
Kevin, when it must be colder up so high than it was
crouching down in a corner of the deck. But Owen was
right, it was fascinating.

Along with the wind shifts came rougher seas. By late
afternoon, the ship was tossing so that Kevin did not see
how anyone could know which way they were going. But
the sailors seemed calm enough, although those aloft had
tied themselves to the masts. In the late afternoon, the
Master of the *Prudence*, Captain Coppin, came on deck
and called all of the passengers to a meeting. After some
pleasantries and introductions, he got down to listing all

the rules for the passengers.

Kevin's ears pricked up when the captain started telling them what to expect that night. "Entering the North Atlantic," he said, "is always a bit rough in the winter. But the bad news is that there seems to be a storm coming in off the roaring forties. We may be able to skirt it if we beat the storm through St. George's Channel, but it might be a little rough the next few days. Now, there's nothing to worry about, but we will require all passengers to stay below decks in rough weather and heavy seas. I'll have no fires of any kind below decks except for two lanterns, and the lanterns must be out by nine o'clock. Remember now, no passengers on deck in a storm. We can't go spinning around the Atlantic like a whirlygig picking up everyone who happens to fall overboard. Now, I'd like to advise you all to eat and get below, and remember, a little seasickness never killed anyone."

Kevin's stomach was in knots already, and the news of a coming storm did little to relax him. When it began to rain, he went below and lay down on his bunk. Tom and most of the others were there as well, none feeling very well from the look of things. The hold already smelled of seasickness, and the lamps kept swinging back and forth casting shadows that too rhythmically reared and then disappeared. Even lying still on his bunk, Kevin felt as if he, too, were swaying back and forth. He rolled over on his stomach and clamped his arms around the narrow bunk frame. Soon Tom and Kevin were sharing a slop pail as they discovered that they too were landlubbers.

The wind had become southerly, and Kevin imagined

it ripping over the Welsh mountains, descending on them ice-cold and angry. He remembered earlier having told Brian that they would be able to see Mount Snowdon before sunset, and how they had looked forward to that. Not now. Not only was it cold in the steerage compartment, but it seemed drafty. Kevin wondered how a ship that would let the wind in could hold out the water. The ship even sounded like it was about to fall apart. With each roll there was a tremendous groaning of timber all around them—loud enough to make Kevin hold his ears against the noise. The first part of his seasickness over, Kevin lay back on his bunk.

"Is it that miserable you are, Kevin?" groaned Tom from his bunk.

"Indeed. I mind the schoolmaster telling me that crossing the Atlantic in the dead of winter would be no game at all, but no one said that it was ever this bad between the islands themselves."

"Aye," chimed in Mr. Donohue, "it was hardly prudent of the *Prudence* to be setting out in the face of such a storm. Don't mind my pun, but I wonder what they were thinking at all."

Just then Owen swung himself into the hold. Someone above battened the hatch after him. Soaked to the skin, Owen did not appear sick in the least. Nor did he wobble or cling to the bunk posts when the ship rolled or pitched.

"We're about to round Holyhead," he announced, then, "Whew, it stinks down here."

"And a merry St. Thomas' day to you too," said Rose coming up with a towel and some dry clothes. "Sure I'm not your own mother, God rest her soul, but you must be minding me when I tell you to come in. It's nigh on two hours you've been out since the rain began falling. It's dead you'll be if you keep up such doings. Now put these on."

"I was wearing the rain gear they gave me," said Owen as he put on the clothes behind a blanket hung between two bunks, "but it seems that their last cabin boy was a head or two taller than myself. But it's all right, because the sailmaker says he can take them up to fit me when he's got the time."

"God have mercy on the boy," said Rose, feeling Owen's forehead. "He must have been driven mad by the lightning. You can't *like* it out there!"

Just then the ship rolled and the hold was filled with the noise of grinding timbers. Everyone held their ears while trying to stay upright. Owen laughed.

"All right, what in the name of St. Pat is it you find so funny?" demanded Brian Ruadh. "From the sounds this overgrown *curragh* is making, you'll be needing to turn into a fish instead of a sailor." Brian was still angry because of the snubs he had received from the sailors when Owen was so obviously their pet. But Brian's pale face, chalky in the lantern light beneath his red hair, showed that his greater emotion at that moment was stark fear.

"Oh, she'll not be breaking up, Brian," said Owen. "What's making all the racket is these bunks you're lazing about on. Seeing as we're really just replacing ballast in an empty hold, they build all these racks out of the cheapest new wood. That's why they creak so. The noise is for your own comfort, so to speak."

Pegeen O'Grady chuckled, but Mr. O'Mallory said in a stern voice, "It seems to me, Owen Morgan, that you'd be taking the part of the ocean against us. These people have never set foot on a ship and it's a new world to them, as by rights it ought to be for you. How is it you've gotten your sea legs and you never out of a potato patch before in all your short life?"

"I'd like to be hearing about that too," said Kevin, no longer able to contain his sentiments. "And what are you about, hobnobbing with these English sailors and all? It wasn't two weeks ago you were ready to slit the throats of the whole nation itself."

Everyone was quiet, and for a minute the ship seemed to stop in mid-roll, leaving the lantern above Owen hanging at an odd angle. Owen took a deep breath and sighed. "I've got to admit, I keep thinking it's strange myself," he said. "But it's not like they're really English—nor American nor Scot nor anything at all for that matter. It's like they belong to no country, or maybe to all of them. Anyway, I can't explain it. It's just that I felt the same way as soon as ever we were floating free in Wexford harbor—as if I'd just come home."

"You must have been born on a ship and never told of it," said someone.

"He's fay," said Brian O'Mallory. And Kevin agreed. Or maybe it was love.

The *Prudence* never succeeded in rounding Holyhead. The storm came howling in off the Atlantic, sweeping up between Wales and Ireland with a great fury. The *Prudence* put in to Cemaes Bay, and tried to ride out the storm in the lee of that northernmost point of Wales. After two days of constant battering in the gale, Captain Coppin ordered the ship home for minor repairs and reprovisioning. The *Prudence* practically flew back to the mouth of the Mersey before the storm winds. Then, for nine days, the passengers and crew watched the storm's handiwork as several battered vessels came limping into the harbor. Standing on deck with Kevin and Owen, Mr. MacBride had the last word on their situation. "Much as I like a good fight with a storm," he said, "being bored is better than being dead." The boys had to agree. But the experience did have its good points. Kevin had gotten his sea legs; when they left Liverpool again on January 8, 1834, almost no one was seasick.

This time, Kevin was almost as active on the ship as Owen, though he could not say that he shared Owen's love of the sea. He still kept clear of those sailors who were most obviously English, but he found Owen had been right about that too. Life on the sea with men of many nationalities had leveled both the speech habits and nationalistic attitudes of most of the sailors, to a point that Kevin found eerie. To Owen, on the other hand, it came naturally. Perhaps it was the Welsh heritage of his parents, or maybe the fact that he had been so suddenly deprived of them. At any rate, it was a question that bothered Kevin for many years after. Even Brian Ruadh seemed a bit more comfortable on board now that the sea was calm, but he was willing to hate the English sailors whether they sounded like cockney lads or Caribbean pirates.

Tom and the rest of the passengers seemed grateful

enough that there was no storm to drive them below, and soon settled into routines that would last most of the trip. This time, when they rounded Holyhead and veered south, the three boys were perched on the foremast shroud about fifteen feet above the deck, which was as high as Mr. MacBride would let them go. Tom stood on the fo'c'sle below them, looking to the southwest where his Mary would stay waiting for him for who knew how long. Brian pulled out his tin whistle and, with one arm around a thick shroud rope, began playing a hornpipe he had learned from one of the sailors. Wales was receding from them as the *Prudence* put out for more open waters.

"That's just the right music," said Owen. "We'll not be seeing land again for a month or more."

Kevin spat once more in the direction of England. Kevin had to agree with Owen that the ocean seemed like a different country—no matter whose flag was above them—and a cleaner place, and more free, than either Ireland or England at the moment. Still, Kevin knew that he was no sailor, and his thoughts were already busy wondering what they would find in Texas. Late that day, when they finally passed out of St. George's Channel into the Atlantic, Kevin cheered with everyone else. The sun was bright on the western sea and the wind was fresh. They were on their way.

# Chapter 6

# Long Days at Sea

Life on board the *Prudence* soon settled into a routine. Everyone was roused at seven in the morning. The ship's rules were that, before the women could even begin to make breakfast, all the bedding had to be rolled and stowed, the steerage compartment swept, and the slop jars emptied. Not that these chores took much time. Since the passengers were hardly fond of the smell between decks (by morning the air was so stale that even the lamps looked dim), everyone pitched in. When the hold had been closed up for more than a day during heavy seas, the stench was almost unbearable. Fortunately, the weather had been mostly fine since their first dismal false start.

Meals were cooked over large open grates on the upper deck. At first, nothing seemed to turn out edible; it was either burned or not completely done. The coal made a hotter fire than the peat most of the women had cooked over all their lives. Anything baked in a dutch oven was generally overdone, but cooking over the fire in an open pan was worse. The wind tended to cool the pans and nearly always succeeded in covering the food with ashes. Still, everyone was grateful for hot meals of any quality, since no fires could be lit during heavy weather.

All the boys expected to feel unusually well fed since Mr. Donohue had bid them feel free with his jerky. The two large barrels of smoked beef he had brought along would last them all the way to Texas. Getting used to such a diet, however, proved as uncomfortable as had acquiring sea legs. Having lived most of their lives on potatoes and stews made with only a few ounces of meat, the boys became reacquainted with the ship's slop jars.

Captain Coppin seemed a stern man from his looks, but he made no objection to letting the boys play in the lower parts of the shrouds. So, much of each day was spent by the boys above the deck. From there they could watch for whales and dolphins, and try to identify the colors of the few ships they passed. When the cry, "Sail Ho!" came from the watch above them, they made a game of it to see who could spot it first. Brian Ruadh usually won at this, so Kevin and Owen teased him that they had been blinded by his hair. But the novelty of such games soon wore off, and after a week of plain sailing they were almost as bored as the other immigrants.

The women sewed and gossipped. Without their villages around them, however, they soon found that they had little to gossip about. The men spent their days pacing the deck and smoking their pipes. They too ran short of things to talk about other than what they were going to do when they got to Texas. Since Mr. Power was coming on a later ship, the men had no one to address their questions to, and questions without answers led to silent meditations. The high point of the day for everyone was just after supper. As if they were relaxing after a hard day's work, the passengers settled back to tell and listen to stories and songs. Sometimes there was even a little music and dancing—mostly the younger women and girls, arms stiff to their sides, concentrating on the intricate footwork and trying to avoid slipping on the moving deck.

It was after such an evening that Kevin was thinking about the stories of old Ireland. Everyone knew that the Irish were great lovers of poetry and tales, but what seemed strange to Kevin was that here, among twenty or more Irish families, Mr. O'Mallory was the only person who knew many of the really *old* tales. Going over to where Mr. Donohue and Brian O'Mallory were lounging by the dull embers of the cooking fire, Kevin asked Mr. O'Mallory how he had come to know so many of the ancient stories.

"Well, I'd like to be saying there was a poet, a *filid*, in my family somewheres," Mr. O'Mallory said, "and that such things had been handed down to me from one father to the next, proper like. But the truth of it is that I just picked them up here and there. You can always tell when a story is really old. I don't know how, but you can, and whenever I hear something of that sort it just sticks in my memory. There's a proper way of saying them though, which I've never been after getting the way of. For one thing, most of the oldest stories have bits of poetry strung

all through them, and I was never a great hand at remembering verse. But what makes you ask, lad?"

"It's leaving Eire and all that, sir," replied Kevin. "I'd
hate to be forgetting or never even hearing all the stories
of old Ireland. There's miles of books about St. Patrick and
Brigid and even Columcille, but I never heard that anyone
ever made a book of the old tales of Fergus and Cuchulain
and Deirdre—or even the little tales about the doings of
the leprechauns. It's like our music. Did you ever see an
Irish musician reading music off a page? No. They've got
the music inside of themselves. I was just thinking that if I
wanted to be able to tell my children about such things, I'd
better be learning them myself."

"That's the very thing I'm ever after telling my Brian
Ruadh, but he's too busy to listen. But there are books of
the stories, aren't there, Patrick?"

"Aye, there are," said Mr. Donohue. "I've seen some
myself. They're in very, very old manuscript, or hand-
written, books in the libraries of the great houses or in
Trinity College in Dublin. And some scholars have copied
a few of them out and had them printed in books you can
buy right now in the bookstalls of Dublin city. But Kevin,
what's all this about children and story-telling? It's a grand-
father you sound like, and you wanting to go soldiering
against the English."

Nat MacBride had just joined the group. "There's lots
of ways to be fighting the English," said the First Mate,
"and keeping the ways and tales of Ireland alive is one of
them. Take Boston for example, or parts of Australia. It's
like someone brought along a pot of shamrocks and St.

Pat's staff itself to bless the land with—it's that Irish they are. Of course, it's the poor part that's Irish, but that'll change. England can't hold on to the Isle forever, and when the time comes to break the ties, Ireland will be needing help from her sons and daughters all over the world. Learn the tales, Kevin, and tell them to your children like my father told them to me. That's how you can help Ireland."

"That's a fine fair speech you're after making," said Mr. O'Mallory, "but I thought you were more American than Irish."

"That I am," said Nat, "and there's no place on the earth as free as the United States, nor likely to be for a long time. It breeds good, free, strong citizens out of men just like yourselves—no offense meant. But look at Andy Jackson. His father was a potato farmer like yourselves, and now he's the President. Or take the man I was named after, Nat Bowditch. Nary a lick of schooling but what he taught himself. He became just about the most famous mathematician around—found mistakes in Newton, he did. And he found so many mistakes in Moore's book on navigation, that was done up by the king's astronomer, that he decided to rewrite the whole book. And what did he do with all his brains? Every time he took ship, he spent all of his free time teaching the men before the mast some navigation so they could move on up to being second mates. He taught my father, in fact, on a long voyage to Manila—my old Da, who could barely even read. And then my Da taught me, using Bowditch's own book. That's what America is all about; that's democracy for you."

Later that night, Owen and Kevin watched as Mr. MacBride used his sextant to take a lunar reading of their longitude. Soon they were plying him with questions which he answered as simply as he could. First, he explained the relationship of the earth to the sun, then the moon to the earth. Soon he had Kevin holding a lantern to represent the sun, and Owen turning a small cannonball representing the earth, while Mr. MacBride moved a smaller ball of string around the cannonball like the moon. They kept at it until the boys had a fair idea of how all that combined motion could tell them exactly where they were in the middle of the ocean. By the time they were finished, the sky had clouded over enough to prevent Mr. MacBride from taking his lunar.

"A few years ago, that would have been a terrible thing," he told them, "missing your lunar like that. Before Bowditch figured out an easier way of doing it, you had to wait for a night when the moon would cross the path of a very bright star. If the star was too dim, or it was too cloudy, you couldn't take your reading. You could go a whole voyage knowing only your latitude from the daytime readings. Now we just sight the moon when it gets between any three stars, and figure it out. That's the hard part for me—the figuring takes me about an hour. My Da said that Bowditch could do it in his head though, and it only took him a couple of minutes."

The next day, Kevin and Owen tried to explain it all to Brian Ruadh, but only ended up confusing themselves. Brian was incredulous at all this talk about the sun and moon and how the earth was sitting at an angle, but decided that he, too, would watch Mr. MacBride use his sextant. After an entire afternoon of telling each other how it all had to work, the boys had a great many questions for Mr. MacBride. Once again he had to explain it using the lantern, a cannonball, and a ball of string. At last even Brian had it down. Using the sextant though, was even more difficult than understanding what it was measuring. The first mate gave each boy a chance to sight the moon and a star through the gleaming brass instrument. Even on a calm night, the boys found out, the deck of a ship moves a great deal.

"It's just a skill," Mr. MacBride reassured them, "like shoeing a skittish horse, I imagine, or shooting a running deer. It's just another way of making your hands and eyes work at the same time. You'll get the hang of it before too long."

"I'm no great hand at using your sextant, Mr. Mac-Bride," said Kevin, "but our schoolmaster always said I had a good head for figures. If it wouldn't be troubling you too much, would you mind at all if I watched you work out the arithmetic for all this?"

"And myself, could I watch too?" asked Owen.

"Sure, I've got the time," said the First Mate, "and what about you, Brian the Red?"

"I think you're all cracked," said Brian to Owen and Kevin. "Weren't we the gay ones when we were quit of school and doing lessons and all? It's not to be starting all that again that I'm going to Texas, and little use of it I'd be getting anyway. What good's all that blather going to do me when I'm busy fighting Indians and building up a farm with my Da and Ma? I think I'd as soon be asleep as filling up my brain with such stuff."

Kevin could see some sense in that. What they really needed, he thought, was someone who could tell them about what grew well in Texas, or teach them Spanish, or something else useful. Navigation might be well and good for Owen, for it looked like Owen would never set foot in Texas. But what good was it for himself and Brian? It was knowledge, he told himself, and the schoolmaster had always said that any kind of knowledge was good. Besides, the arithmetic would help him with the business side of farming. But Mr. MacBride brought up something else.

"What use indeed?" he said to Brian. "Don't you know that navigation is only the backside of surveying? If you can learn to make your way around the ocean, then you can surely tell whether someone is cheating you on a property line. Or maybe you can get a job on a surveying team and go out exploring that wilderness you're headed for."

Brian gave in to that, saying if you could earn money doing it, then it must be useful. Soon they were down in Mr. MacBride's cabin, looking at maps of the stars and of the ocean, comparing long columns of numbers in Bowditch's *Navigation*, and listening to the First Mate explain all sorts of mathematics which they had never heard of before.

After that, the boys spent every night Mr. MacBride could spare learning all they could about navigation. Owen finally got permission from Rose and from Captain Coppin, to stay on board the *Prudence* as cabin boy. He applied himself to the task of learning to steer by the stars as if he were going to pilot the ship back across the Atlantic all by himself. Brian, on the other hand, kept interrupting their sessions to ask questions about how all this would be done on land. Kevin just tried to soak it all in. One way or another, he told himself, it would be useful.

What with learning navigation most nights, and prying more stories out of Mr. O'Mallory during the day, Kevin had his time well filled. For Tom, however, the days went by slowly. He spent most of his time pacing or sitting with the other men, talking about nothing for hours at a time and generally getting more and more restless. To Kevin he seemed downright grouchy, ready to tell Kevin just how little he knew about farming or fighting or anything. It seemed that Tom now thought that Kevin would be worse than useless in Texas, which made Kevin both sad and angry. They argued more than once, with Tom saying it was just like Kevin to be wasting his time memorizing stories and learning navigation when he could be useful. Of course, Kevin could see little "useful" that Tom was doing, and told him so.

"Mooning up and down like a love-sick cow," he said, "that's all you've done for weeks."

"You leave my love life out of this," Tom said. "You've embarrassed Mary and me too many times with your barefoot antics and all your tagging along when I was courting her."

Of course, that wasn't fair and Kevin felt it. Still, he knew that Tom was worried about Mary. She was a strong willed girl and might take it into her head to get on a ship at any time and follow them—or what was worse, she might up and marry some other fellow. Kevin knew that was nonsense, but he could see that to Tom it was a terrible risk, whether or not she had vowed to stay true to him. In short, Tom had become a real pain to live with in the middle of the ocean on a small ship taking him ever farther from his auburn-haired beauty.

Thus Kevin was almost happy when, as they were about to enter the Caribbean, Captain Coppin announced that they were being followed. The passengers had noticed a day or two back when the watch had called out a sail several times in one afternoon. They discussed it all evening, some saying that they must have crossed a shipping lane, some fearing that they were being chased by pirates. That fear was confirmed when the captain requested that anyone having a firearm on board should unpack and clean it. Everyone was immediately roused from the stupor of the last few lazy weeks, including Tom. He was ready to turn and fight until he learned that there were only three small cannon on board. The ship's armory contained a mere ten rifles and very little shot and powder. Among the immigrants, only four weapons were produced. This was hardly surprising though, since it had been illegal for the Irish to possess firearms of any sort for time out of mind.

Pegeen O'Grady, former mistress of the Vinegar Hill Tavern in Enniscorthy, produced the only modern gun, a flintlock derringer with two barrels. Mr. Donohue showed off his great-great-grandfather's matchlock blunderbuss pistol. It was still an admirably wicked weapon for a single shot, but very heavy and slow to fire. Still, everyone thought it a pretty thing with its silver fittings and engraved steel barrel. Another passenger, William St. John, had a set of wheel lock duelling pistols, but both were rusted and the crank was missing. Repairing and cleaning Mr. St. John's pistols gave the men something to do the rest of the afternoon. They talked on and on about various guns they had seen or used or just heard about. And of course, there were plenty of pirate stories.

When everyone had just about scared themselves to death, Captain Coppin and Mr. MacBride came forward to see how they were getting on with the guns. The Captain seemed more interested in the old guns than he was in the pirates. Finally, Tom asked the question which everyone wanted answered.

"Captain Coppin, sir," said Tom, "we've been hearing

a great lot of tales this day about pirates, Blackbeard and Henry Morgan and that lot. Who is it we'd be facing in that ship behind us?"

Captain Coppin gave a laugh. "Oh, no one as cruel or famous as that," he said. "The last pirate in these waters to make a name for himself was Jean Lafitte, who helped Andy Jackson in the war at New Orleans. But he's dead now and his band is scattered all along the Texas coast. They say he buried treasures all along the coast from the Neches to the Lavaca. That's right near where you'll be settling. But if the folk astern are pirates, it's most likely they're looking for ships carrying specie or Mexican silver. If they catch sight of a lot of Irish farmers on deck, they'll know we wouldn't be worth their time."

"It's not like it used to be on the Spanish Main," said Mr. MacBride, "with Her Majesty's privateers out hunting the Spaniards, and the Spanish hunting the English, and buccaneers burying the treasure of both sides. Pirates these days can be just as murderous, but they're not nearly so bold."

After that, the Captain asked the boys to go aloft again and sit in the foremast shroud. "No one," he said, "could mistake us for anything but an immigrant ship if they see a bunch of landlubbers lazing all over the ship." So the boys went aloft again—or at least they went as high aloft as the sailors would let them. Behind the *Prudence*, the sail no longer disappeared over the horizon; it was gaining. The boys stayed until it became too dark to see.

Anxiety reached a high point the next morning when it could be seen clearly by everyone that the following ship was overtaking them. Captain Coppin was constantly ordering the Irish women away from the stern because they interfered with his helmsman. Shading their eyes with their shawls pulled over their heads, the women clustered at the railings, clucking and squawking like so many frightened hens. It was about noon when the ship suddenly veered south, off the track of the *Prudence*, without the watchman ever having identified her colors.

There was a great sense of relief as the passengers, crowded to the port side, watched the pirate ship (all the passengers felt sure it had been pirates) sail away to the south. But relief also meant a return to boredom. This was short-lived though, as the Captain announced the next day that they had rounded Florida during the night, and would be in New Orleans in just a few days. Everyone began preparing their things as if they would go ashore the very next day. The women finished up what they were sewing; the men finished their whittling. Kevin spent the time thinking about the tales and poetry he had memorized and the navigation he had learned.

When they were well into the Gulf of Mexico, Kevin could fairly *feel* the Americas around him. Although these waters were well traveled, it seemed to Kevin that he could sense the strangeness of the lands ahead. Occasionally the *Prudence* came near enough to the shore that it could be seen through Mr. MacBride's spyglass. It looked like a jungle—not at all what Kevin or anyone else had been expecting. The tree line along those sandy shores looked like a dark green wall, hung with vines and moss. It was as forbidding a place as Kevin ever wished to see. The sailors told them stories of alligators that could bite a man in half and of deadly snakes that would drop down on a person from out of the trees; they told them about track-less swamps and bayous, and about mosquitoes an inch long.

Last of all, the passengers were regaled with tales of the high life to be had in New Orleans. It took most of an afternoon for Mr. MacBride to calm the fears of the gullible immigrants. He described New Orleans as a wealthy, cul-tured, port city with an opera and good hotels. One of the hands who had actually seen the coast of Texas told them that it was much different from what they had seen. The sailor had heard more than he had seen, however, and began telling those clustered around him how the Texas coast was infested with cannibals before Mr. MacBride sent him to the galley. The First Mate was kept busy reas-suring the future colonists that Texas was not the end of the world. From all that he had heard, he told them, the first few miles inland were indeed marshy, but beyond that the land was very much like Ireland. Even if the interior had been heaven itself, it would not have made much difference in the way folk slept in the hold of the *Prudence* that night. More than a few people awoke with night-mares, not all of them children.

There was no telling what lay in store for them ashore, but sailing the Gulf was delightful. A good breeze gave them steady speed, and the seas were much calmer than the Atlantic had been even in good weather. The tempera-ture was pleasant, but Kevin had an idea that without the wind it would be warmer than any February of his life. The summer that was coming in this latitude might be awesomely hot. Sitting in their favorite places on the foremast shroud, Kevin, Owen, and Brian talked about what they had seen and heard and what they felt about the new land. Owen, for one, was overjoyed that he would not have to face any alligators or snakes. Brian did not relish that prospect either, but said that it was better than being seasick all of one's life.

"Ah, Brian, it isn't seasick you've been for nearly a month," said Kevin.

"But what about living your whole life," Brian retorted, "not knowing whether the next sail you see on the horizon will be a ship full of pirates ready to slit your throat for the fun of it—and you with only a few wee cannon and guns that ought to be in museums. And what about being out on the trackless ocean for months at a time with the only way of knowing where you are at all being a chancy look at the stars and an hour of arithmetic? No, give me good dry land any day, snakes and all, where you can see where you're going and can tell who's your friend or enemy."

Looking back on it, Kevin had enjoyed the voyage much more than he had thought he would at first. His only regret was that Owen would not be going on to Texas with them. It was still a mystery to Kevin how Owen could forget so soon what the English had done to his family. Most of the sailors were either English or Scots, and he had never been able to feel comfortable around those few who were openly pro-British and Protestant. Yet Owen seemed friendly with all of them. Even if he did not understand how Owen could stomach the company, Kevin could see that he would never be happy anywhere but on the sea. You could see it in everything he did, even the way he moved.

"Be happy for him," Tom told Kevin. "It's not often a lad of his age gets to do what God meant him to do. He probably would have been miserable if he'd lived his whole life on dry land—and himself never knowing the cause of his misery. It's that lucky he is to have found himself on a boat with a kind master and a willing teacher."

And so it was that, on a windy day in February, Kevin and Owen parted. They had docked at New Orleans, and their baggage had been transferred to a warehouse where it would stay until the remainder of the colonists had arrived from Ireland. Owen had already said his goodbyes to the rest of the party, especially to the Donohues who had brought him away with them as if he had been their own son. Tom, Kevin, Brian, and Owen stood near the gangway of the *Prudence*.

"Kevin," said Owen, "I know that you think it's strange that I'm not always ranting about the English and what they've done to me, but don't think that I'm after forgetting it. It's just that I've found something to do, something I love, to give me a place in the world. But if you're ever going back to Eire with that army of yours, count me in."

It was that simple, thought Kevin, as they shook hands and gave each other a hug. It was really like Mr. MacBride had said: the best way to help Ireland was to carry the Isle around with you, in your heart and in your head, until the right moment came again to give it your body. Owen was like that; he'd be ready when the time came, and much more valuable for the waiting.

When Owen was back aboard the *Prudence*, the three boys turned from the docks and walked back into the city of New Orleans. In only a few days, they would all wish that they too were sailing back across the Atlantic.

*Chapter 7*

# Death in New Orleans

It was uncertain how long the Irish colonists would have to remain in New Orleans. Mr. Power had chartered another ship, the *Heroine*, to bring over a much larger group of people than had sailed on the *Prudence*, but no one had been sure of its sailing date when they left Liverpool. Most of Kevin's group expected the *Heroine* to arrive within the month, at which time they could go on to Texas all together with Mr. Power as their guide. Meanwhile, the colonists had taken up lodgings in various apartments near the river. The rooms were small, but not nearly so filthy as those they had been forced to take in Liverpool. After a day or two of vigorous scrubbing, most found them a pleasant contrast to the cramped and airless quarters aboard the *Prudence*.

New Orleans turned out to be everything it had been described, whether by the crew of the *Prudence* or by her First Mate. There was, in fact, an opera with a small orchestra. There were also several fine hotels. But it was also a river town with plenty of open bars and gambling houses with huge chandeliers. Inside these places the women wore their skirts slit higher up the sides than the Irish believed God would allow. Some of the streets were cobbled, some paved with brick, some were dirt. They were lined with fine houses and hovels, smelly livery stables and smellier fish markets, auction platforms, warehouses, and shops of every description.

If the city itself was fascinating to the colonists, watching its inhabitants became an almost hypnotic occupation among them. At all hours and on every street in the city, there was a parade of humanity such as these folk of the quiet Irish countryside had never imagined: sailors, soldiers, river rats, and gentlemen; black, white, and red; ladies of the evening and street vendors. The colonists watched them all, trying to find their own place in this new world.

Kevin and Tom spent whole days walking the streets, listening and watching, and asking questions whenever they found someone willing to answer them. Tom seemed a lot less grumpy than he had on the ship. Probably, thought Kevin, because Tom was just as awed by their new surroundings as Kevin. Still, Tom would never admit that, and Kevin was annoyed that his older brother wouldn't let him go out in the city by himself. In the meantime, they couldn't help but share in the excitement of being in such a strange new place among its even stranger inhabitants.

After a few days, they agreed that by far the most

intriguing characters they had seen were the men from the far west, dressed in their Indian garb. These trappers and hunters had roamed the farthest reaches of the continent. They wore buckskin pants and shirts covered by woolly buffalo coats or thick, coarsely woven ponchos. A poncho was basically a blanket with a hole in the middle for one's head—a simple affair usually, except for the distinctive geometric patterns woven in them. Their buckskins were generally slick with suet and buffalo grease—to make them waterproof, one man told Kevin—and smelled to high heaven. Every seam of their clothing had long leather fringe hanging from it. The fringe was used as an instant source of string, Kevin was told, and new clothes were made when a man ran out of fringe. Some of the mountain men, however, wore a finer sort of buckskin,

softer and lighter in color, and usually covered in Indian bead or quill work. The quills, they said, came from an animal called a porcupine. These were dyed, flattened, and woven into geometric designs.

Tom thought these clothes were gaudy, but he didn't dare laugh at the men wearing them. As a rule, the mountain men were taller than anyone else in the city. Kevin thought that both the men and their clothes were very impressive, and determined that he would start wearing leather clothes too—at the first opportunity.

The trappers and hunters were mostly silent men, but occasionally Kevin and Tom would hear one telling tales of the life he led when away in the west. And what tales! Huge bears with claws a foot long lurked behind every rock, murderous mountain lions crept stealthily in the night, Indians lay waiting to take your scalp. And the land, they said, was just as strange as its inhabitants were dangerous. Kevin heard story after story about glass mountains, boiling springs, trees in far California with trunks as big around as houses, and whole forests made of stone. But such things were far away. Texas, they said, was heaven except for the Comanches, some of the wildest Indians around. Tom and Kevin talked more than once about going west and making their fortunes as fur trappers, but in their hearts they knew that their roles were already cast for them. Still, it was exciting to think about roaming the wilder lands to the west.

In their rooms at night, the colonists would gather to talk about all they had seen and worry about the arrival of the *Heroine.* Often they told of horrifying scenes they had witnessed at the auction blocks where black men, women, and children were sold as slaves. Their own oppression under England was nothing compared to the degradation of these folk from Africa, chained like wild animals and regarded as such. The colonists heard many arguments in favor of slavery, such as it being really the best possible thing for the slaves since they would become civilized and eventually Christians. But it did not sit well with the Irish, and did not seem to fit at all into Nat MacBride's glowing description of American democracy. The colonists were genuinely glad that they were going on to Texas where their colony would be isolated, their few neighbors Catholics like themselves.

One evening in early March, Mr. Donohue was reading to the group from the newspaper. The news was ominous. Sweeping across the southern United States was an epidemic of cholera which might reach New Orleans any day. The very next morning, Kevin saw hundreds of people leaving town. The docks were crowded with people waiting to be ferried across the Mississippi, and the northern roads were jammed with people leaving.

The colonists were not immune to fear, and several families decided that they would rather make their way to the colony on foot than risk playing a waiting game between the arrival of the epidemic and the *Heroine*. Pegeen O'Grady bought herself a wagon and a bigger pistol and set out with about ten others. Sadly, they bade their fellow travelers farewell.

Mr. Donohue had refused to exchange his silver pounds for dollars in Liverpool, fearing that the exchange rate would not be in his favor. As a consequence, he found himself to be fairly well off in New Orleans. Silver was silver, they said, no matter how you cut it. Expecting the arrival of the *Heroine* any day, and with plenty of cash in his pockets, Mr. Donohue suggested that they move to one of the better hotels. It would be cleaner, he told them, and would have a doctor on call if the worst happened. They all agreed, and made the move that very day. Even though Mr. Donohue offered to get rooms for Brian O'Mallory and his family, they decided to stay where they were. There were fewer occupants in the building now, and Mrs. O'Mallory refused to take any more kindnesses from her sister until, as she put it, she could "be borrowing Margaret's menfolk to be raising a new roofbeam." Within two weeks, Mr. and Mrs. O'Mallory were dead.

The epidemic broke around them like the huge ocean waves had broken over the deck of the *Prudence*. Once again Kevin had a feeling of isolation combined with fear born of ignorance. It was as if the hotel which only yesterday seemed so vast—had suddenly become the dark cramped quarters of a ship being tossed about in a storm. No one knew for sure how cholera was transmitted, but a favorite theory was that it was somehow related to a "bad atmosphere." To purge the atmosphere, cauldrons of burning tar and pitch were set out in the streets, covering the city with a dense black cloud. No one dared venture outside unless it was absolutely necessary, and the streets looked strange and desolate without their usual bustling crowds.

Mr. Donohue's move to the hotel had certainly given them cleaner surroundings and better food, but the hotel doctor was reluctant to treat the immigrants, whom he claimed had played some part in bringing the disease to America. Soon Mr. and Mrs. Donohue fell ill with the cholera. The doctor proclaimed them both light cases, gave them some calomel to clear their intestines, and went his way. Amazingly, his diagnosis proved correct. In a few days, looking drawn and very weak, both were on the way to recovery. Kevin was not so lucky. The disease had no common course. You could "wake up dead," as they said, or you could fight it for weeks. Kevin fought it.

At the first sign of the disease, Kevin was put in a room by himself. It seemed to him that he would never stop throwing up. Then he was too weak to even get up to relieve himself. There were long days and nights of muscle cramps, beginning in his stomach and radiating out to his limbs. He became too weak to resist them and, lying drawn up in a ball, at last lost all consciousness of anything that was going on around him. Tom and Rose Donohue, if Kevin had known it, tended him day and night. They kept him warm with blankets and sheets which had to be boiled or burned as soon as they were soiled, and bathed him constantly with wet cloths. He was given huge doses of calomel to "cleanse his system," and even larger doses of mineral water mixed with salt and soda to replace the water the calomel forced out of him.

It was mid-April before Kevin was aware that he was back among the living, and it was two more weeks before he could manage to walk the length of the hallway outside his room. Rose had been responsible for Kevin's treatment after she decided that she knew more about the disease than the doctor. "Whether it be a wee bug that you can't be seeing at all," she said, "like they say brings on the smallpox, or the 'atmospheric disturbance' these high sounding doctors are always talking about, or even the curse of God Almighty that they're preaching in the streets below, I'd rather be trusting my own common sense over all them folks' fancy notions."

So Kevin spent the last two weeks of April sitting in the open air of the second floor veranda, soaking up the ever warmer sunshine and breathing the thick humid air. Brian was with them now. After his parents had died—very quickly, he told Kevin, but would say no more—he had seen them buried in a local Catholic cemetery for the poor.

"Ah, Kevin," he said, although Tom and Rose were standing by them, "how is it that God could bring them across that great length of ocean and be setting them down safe here, and let them go on making their grand dreams, and them not knowing at all what was around the corner? How could He take them after all their work to be getting here?"

"There's no answer for that, Brian Ruadh O'Mallory," said Rose. "But your Ma and Da, God rest their souls, were not the only ones to be taken that way. Over half the folk that were our fellow travelers on the *Prudence* have died here with the same great dreams as your own father and mother. It's only for the sake of you three boys, I'm thinking, that God in His mercy brought my own parents back from the edge of death."

With one arm on Brian's shoulder and the other around Tom's waist, Rose said, "Don't you be worrying now. The Donohues will see you safe to Texas, just like we promised you and your folks we would. We'll be getting to Texas and starting a new life and putting all this misery behind us."

During the long days of Kevin's recovery, Tom and Brian brought him up to date on things that had happened during his sickness. On April 20, the *Prudence* had docked again. Tom had been the one to break the news of the epidemic to Captain Coppin and the new Irish colonists on board. The colonists had been crushed to be so greeted in the land that held so much hope for them, but had no choice but to go ashore. The *Heroine* had departed Liverpool at the same time as the *Prudence*, and was expected in any day. The *Prudence* lay at anchor for a few days before putting her passengers ashore, but as the *Heroine* did not arrive, the Captain felt he was putting his crew at risk to remain any longer. Few of the crew ever set foot off the ship. Owen had wanted to go see Kevin, but neither Captain Coppin nor Tom would allow it.

When all the passengers had disembarked and their cargo been unloaded, the *Prudence* set sail without even taking on any new cargo, for fear of being struck with the pestilence at sea. Owen had sent his best wishes and blessings to Kevin, and a present. With his first pay (and with a small loan from Mr. MacBride, Kevin found out later) Owen had bought a new rifle for Kevin. It was a fine American rifle, a long flintlock with a stock of maple wood. For his part, Kevin spent the hot days on the veranda fingering the weapon and waiting for the day when he would be strong enough to go somewhere in the woods

where he could try it out.

It was on such an afternoon, on May 10, that news came to them that the *Heroine* was docking, bearing James Power, the impresario of the Irish colony, many members of the Power family, and some 200 new colonists. They were greeted with the news that over half the folk who had preceded them to America were dead, that some had gone on to Texas on foot, and that many more still lay sick. For those who had survived the ordeal in New Orleans, however, the arrival of the *Heroine* could not have been a happier event.

# Part Three

# Chapter 8

# Texas At Last!

James Power was a commanding figure, tall and handsome in his high beaver hat and long-tailed coat. The foot-long brass barrel of a Hollis flintlock pistol gleamed where he carried it stuck into his belt. In a sheath strapped to his leg was an enormous knife. Kevin had seen one like it in a blacksmith's shop in New Orleans. The smithy had called it a Bowie knife because a man named Jim Bowie had made it famous by his skill in fighting with such a blade. It seemed that Bowie, too, had gone to Texas. Kevin imagined that he must be a lot like "Colonel" Power, as everyone here called him.

The impresario had the swagger of a man used to authority. He had emigrated from Ballygarrett to Philadelphia when he was twenty-one, and had travelled the length of the frontier all the way to Mexico. There he had established himself in business and in time had married a señorita of Matamoros, Dolores de la Portilla. He and his father-in-law, Don Felipe Roque de la Portilla, had been impresarios for an earlier settlement deep in Texas on the San Marcos River, but Power had eventually moved to Live Oak Point between Copano and Nueces Bays on the coast, where the Colonel's house was famous locally for the number of its chimneys. Kevin was impressed. Power's commitment to the colony was proven as well. The Colonel's first son had been born on the very day that Power had set out for Ireland. He was ready to sail when the message came, but such was his resolution for the success of the colony that he had sailed without even returning to see his new child.

Although the worst of the cholera epidemic had passed, none of the colonists wished to remain long in New Orleans. Two schooners lay at anchor in the Mississippi, both bound for Texas. The *Wild Cat* had already taken on several non-Irish passengers going to Copano on the Texas coast. Power chartered the remaining space for the immigrants who had had the misfortune to spend the last several months in the disease-ridden frontier town, and had those still aboard the *Heroine* transferred directly to the second schooner, the *Sea Lion*.

The weather had turned hot and sultry. Kevin had never been so uncomfortable in his life and the little strength he had built up was soon sapped. A return to the clean salt breezes of the ocean sounded like heaven to the Irish who had suffered so much in New Orleans. Thus it was that, leaning heavily upon the long rifle given him by Owen, Kevin made his way up the gangplank of the *Wild Cat*. When they weighed anchor the Irish gave an enthusiastic cheer, though few of the voices raised were entirely healthy.

Kevin had learned a great deal about the American lands in the last two months, but still Power's description of the Texas coast as resembling Wexford stayed in his mind, as it did for many of the Irish. Though it made no sense, they half expected the weather to cool as they neared the coast. And it did. All afternoon the colonists crowded the deck, revelling in the fresh air and cool winds. The sailors did not seem half so pleased with the weather as were the passengers, though there was little to be done but sail on. They awoke early the next morning to heavy seas and a building storm. The ship was anchored within sight of the shore.

The news spread quickly and soon everyone was on deck, peering through the curtain of rain which obscured their view of the promised land. It certainly did not look like Ireland. From what they could see, it looked like some desert seacoast with low sandy beaches, bare except for driftwood and a few patches of sea oats. There were no rolling green hills, no trees, nothing but sand and murky, churning water. The Captain of the vessel was too busy to address all the questions of his passengers, but they learned that what they could see was only one of the outer islands. To the south was Mustang Island, to the north, San José. Invisible to the colonists was Aransas Pass, a narrow channel between the two islands which threaded its way west, then north behind San José Island into the open waters of Aransas Bay. On either side were extensive shallows, sand bars, and mud flats. The colonists were

dumbfounded when they heard their Captain begin shouting orders to put on full sail. Later it was explained that
since the channel was so shallow, the high tides and strong
winds gave the *Wild Cat* a better chance of crossing the
bar and entering the bay waters than would have been
possible on a calm day. For the moment, Kevin, Tom,
Brian, and the Donohues stood with the other passengers
fearfully watching the shore grow nearer. The sailors
stayed aloft, ready to reef sail at any moment.

   The sand bars and mudflats were so close about them
that it seemed impossible a ship the size of the *Wild Cat*
could ever navigate there. They could just hear the keel
grating when a heavy swell lifted the ship and carried it
clear of the channel by a few feet. There was a heavy thud
as she settled in about five feet of water and the masts
groaned as they strained against the suddenly still hull.
The next wave was even larger and sprayed across part of
the deck. Again the ship was lifted, this time to even shal-
lower water where it was obvious that she would remain.
For a few minutes even the storm seemed drowned beneath the curses of the sailors and the wailing, like a
banshee's *caoine*, of the Irish women. Soon, however, the
very stillness of the ship had a calming effect and everyone
settled down to watch the storm and await the arrival of
the *Sea Lion*. It was an eerie vigil through the bit of the day
left and all the next night, stuck fast on a still and silent
ship, wrecked halfway between the fury of the ocean and
the dreamed-of lands to the west. Kevin could not sleep at
all, but listened to the women's voices saying rosaries all
through the night.

Early the next morning, two ships were sighted approaching the pass. The first to attempt a crossing turned out to be the *Cardena*, a merchant vessel loaded with goods bound for San Antonio. Attempts by the crew of the *Wild Cat* to direct her into the channel went unheeded because of the fog. The sea was heavier than on the previous day and the *Cardena* ran aground, turned quickly broadside to the sea and wind, and rolled. Within two hours the surf had torn her to pieces. It was a graphic example to the colonists of what their own fate might have been, and their prayers for salvation became prayers of gratitude.

The *Sea Lion* carried most of the colonists, including some of those from the second landing of the *Prudence* and from the *Heroine*. The *Sea Lion* stood off and on until late in the afternoon when the storm had died down slightly. The haze never lifted, however, and again the Irish on board the *Wild Cat* had to witness the folly of trying to cross this bar in such a storm. The master of the *Sea Lion* put on all sail and came swiftly toward the *Wild Cat*. The ship missed the channel by just a few yards on the side opposite that to which the *Wild Cat* had been thrown. There was a tremendous thumping as each roll of the surf pushed the *Sea Lion* a bit farther over the sand bar.

During this ordeal, the ship began to leak, filling the lower hull with water. Just at nightfall, she managed to clear the bar and was free for a moment or two. There was no steering her, however, with a hold full of water and with so much canvas still up. Almost at once the *Sea Lion* settled heavily into a mudbank. For years afterwards, the

*Sea Lion* would remain there, a good source of planking for the settlers' cabins and stores in the small town of Copano, but at last a rotting hulk in a flat plain of mud.

As bad as things seemed to the Irish and other colonists stuck aboard the two intact ships, the morning light brought an even worse disaster. There was cholera aboard the *Sea Lion*. Colonel Power came across in a lifeboat to inform the captain of the *Wild Cat* that he had already been in contact with the Mexican officials at Copano. The officer there refused to let any passengers ashore until the outbreak had passed, which could mean weeks aboard the stranded vessels. Fresh food and water, however, would be provided by the Mexican authorities and by Colonel Power's relatives living nearby.

Kevin was standing beside Tom at the stern railing when they saw the first body thrown from the side of the *Sea Lion*.

"I'm hoping the tide will be carrying the poor souls out into the ocean yonder," Tom said. "If things go here like they did in New Orleans, this backwater will soon be littered with such sights, God have mercy on them."

"Aye," said Kevin, "and maybe our side of this cursed channel as well. I'm just after hearing Rose telling how Mr. St. John's child is unwell—with the fever and vomiting and all."

"It's that bad," said Rose coming up to them. "He has the cholera and no doubt. They're moving him now to keep him isolated, but I doubt he'll make the night."

Rose's prediction was accurate. The next morning two men, a Mr. Priour and Mr. Paul Keogh, took the body of the child over to San José Island, since seeing her child buried at sea was more than Mrs. St. John could stand.

"There's neither priest nor churchyard," she said, "but at least he'll be buried in ground with a holy name on it. I've prayed faithful to St. Joseph all the length of my life; perhaps he'll be tending the soul of my child now as will be buried in the sands of his isle over there."

The two men were gone for more than two days. When Mr. Priour climbed aboard looking haggard and pale, it was clear that he had the sickness as well. Paul Keogh had died of it on the beach. Kevin's group kept to themselves, staying apart from the other colonists and eating only fresh food from the shore which they prepared themselves. Kevin and Brian spent much of their time on one of the lower yardarms. Tom often joined them now as it simply felt safer to be removed, if only by a few feet, from the deck of the death-filled ship. The Donohues spent most of their time as far forward on the prow as they could get without actually climbing onto the bowsprit. Other families followed similar practices, huddling here and there on the deck, shunning the hold at all costs unless one of their own were dying there.

After two weeks, when the sea and the sands of Mustang and San José Islands had received nearly 250 of the colonists and sailors, the epidemic vanished as quickly as it had appeared. The remaining passengers were transported to Copano aboard the schooner *Sabine*, which had passed through the Aransas Pass with little difficulty a few days before. Her Master, Captain Auld, was a kind man who took pity on the lot of the immigrants. He did what he saw as his duty and got both people and goods to shore with dispatch. It was toward the end of May, fully six months since Kevin had watched his family, standing on the Wexford docks, recede into the dim green hills that were the Ireland of his memory. The kindness of Captain Auld brought to mind the brave days Kevin had spent with Owen and Brian on board the *Prudence*, when hope had still sprung from every mouth at the mention of Texas.

Since the *Sabine* was departing in a few days—and the colonists had no idea when they would see a ship again—many of them composed letters to their relatives at home in Ireland to be carried as far as New Orleans by Captain Auld. Kevin wrote a letter for Tom and himself:

*Dearest Mother, Father, Cathleen and Brigid,*

*God bless you all and how we miss you every one. Tom and meself are safe and standing upon the land of Texas itself, this being the first day of June. You will be hearing some terrible sorrowful things about our voyage. Many of friends and fellow passengers have gone to their rest with God in heaven, most taken by the cholera which met us in the city of New Orleans. The disease broke out again before we could disembark here at Copano Bay. In fact, of the 108 souls who set out with us on the Prudence from Liverpool, only 8 are with us now.*

You should know that Mr. and Mrs. O'Mallory were among those who passed on. Brian is healthy, as are Mr. and Mrs. Donohue and Rose, Tom and meself—though they say I was as close to death as I ever care to be in New Orleans. Owen never left the Prudence and is now cabinboy to her captain. That is a strange tale worthy of a long telling, but I have no time for it now as the captain of the vessel is calling for these letters to be put in his strongbox. It is indeed a fair land though we have only just gotten here and have not seen more than the shore. It is very hot but beautiful as well. Pure white shorebirds as tall as meself. So much to tell but I must say farewell. We remember you every hour. Tom sends his love to Mary as well. In Christ,

         Kevin Brendan + Tom John

*Chapter 9*

# Snakes and Alligators

The Mexican authorities at Copano were, at first, neither friendly nor kind. It was obvious that they feared the colonists and the cholera they might still harbor among them. The officer in charge put them under a further quarantine—under guard—on the beach. The shore was littered with oyster shells, long a staple of the Karankawa Indians who were the original inhabitants of the place. Soon the colonists were enjoying feasts of baked oysters almost every night. At least those among them who had a taste for the shellfish were enjoying them.

There was an occasional deer near the shore as well, and with the help of a Mexican soldier and a large group of Irish onlookers, Kevin got to squeeze off the first shot from Owen's rifle. He missed, of course, and he thought that his shoulder would never feel quite in its proper place again, but it was very exciting. It was not long before he had become a pet of the soldiers, who obviously enjoyed shooting the fine rifle as much as Kevin did. Every day they spent several hours firing off musket ball after musket ball at squirrels, swamp rabbits, deer, and once a wild hog. Tom went along as well, and shot as much as Kevin. Because he was larger and could handle the weapon more easily, Tom turned out to be a much better shot than Kevin. Still, by the time their period of quarantine ended, Kevin was reckoned to have become a fair shot even by the soldiers' standards.

Also by that time, the Mexican soldiers had warmed up to the colonists. There was guitar playing at night and some dancing. One or two of the heavy-booted soldiers did a sort of quick stomping dance that made a drum-like sound on the wooden floor of the customshouse. Some of the Irish girls showed off their stiff-armed and light-footed

steps, but on the whole the mood was not a dancing one. There was hardly anyone who was not in mourning for family members or friends. Still, there was a giddy sort of feeling, as if folk were laughing and crying at the same time. The fact of the matter was that, as sad as one might be over the loss of loved ones, it was hard to ignore the sheer relief of knowing that one had survived—that every minute would bring some new word, some new sound, some new sight. When they began their journey inland, the customshouse soldiers seemed truly sad to see them leave.

The next stop for the Irish was the mission of *Nuestra Señora del Refugio*, Our Lady of Refuge. It sounded a fine place, especially since many of the Irish had been without the Blessed Sacrament since their departure from Liverpool, and many had lost loved ones for whom they earnestly desired to pray in the presence of Christ. When they arrived at the mission, however, they reined in their creaking oxcarts before an abandoned structure, constructed of poorly-made adobe which was already beginning to crumble. Vines covered the outer walls and weeds were beginning to grow in the cracks. Inside, the mission was stuffed with provender for the Mexican cavalry detachment stationed a few miles to the north in the *Presidio La Bahía* at Goliad.

The 150 survivors of the Aransas disaster were met at the mission by about a hundred Mexican and seventy other colonists contracted to the Power colony. This large group had little to do but wait while Colonel Power contacted the authorities about issuing titles to their lands. It was a time of anxiety and gathering tension. A crop had to be put in the ground soon if they were to have anything to eat for the winter. It seemed there were always Indians skulking around their possessions piled against the mission walls.

Rumors of all sorts circulated. Many of the rumors concerned the Mexican government. While they were still in Ireland, it had been a great comfort to know that just a few miles to the south of the Power colony was the already-established Irish community of *San Patricio de Hibernia*. This thriving town was part of a colony founded by two Irishmen, James McGloin of County Sligo and John McMullen. Now the Irish at Refugio began to hear tales of how the Mexican government had refused to grant land titles for as long as six years. Many of the new settlers began to grumble that Power had misled them. The land of milk and honey he had described to them in Ireland had given them nothing but death and disaster so far. Now they were hearing that the land promised to them might never be legally theirs.

As for Kevin, Tom, and Brian Ruadh, they were content to let Colonel Power haggle with the Mexicans over legal matters. There was a new land all around them, and they were aching to be off exploring it. Texas was strange and yet familiar all at the same time. It did, in fact, look like parts of Wexford, with its wide green meadows broken only by copses—or *matas*—of oak and mesquite trees. Instead of the land being criss-crossed by hedgerows and stone walls, the gently undulating hills of Texas were webbed with a network of *galerias*, or tree-lined creeks and rivers. In this sense it was all beautiful. But the country could also be hostile and exotic.

In their walks around the Refugio mission, one of the boys was always calling out to the others to come and see some new plant or animal. Kevin was so overwhelmed by the sheer amount of information he learned each day— and the number of questions each new item raised—that he began keeping a record book of everything he saw. In green well-watered meadows there were cactus plants of all descriptions and where there was no apparent water near, Kevin saw rolling fields of rich grasses dotted with flowers of every hue and color. But strangest of all was the wildlife. Huge shaggy buffalo could be seen every now and then, and enormous herds of deer—sometimes as many as a thousand in a single group. When the deer in such a herd began to move, to run and leap, the landscape shimmered as if it were a mirage. There were wild horses in abundance, wild cattle, and wild cats—and birds, birds, birds.

Nearer the coast, Kevin remembered the variety of stiff-legged shore birds delicately picking their way along the water's edge. The gulls had been their travel companions throughout the voyage, but at Copano the gulls had flown side by side with large pelicans, skimming and dipping just above the surface. Once when Kevin and Tom had been out shooting with one of their guards, a black-necked stilt had hovered over them for almost half an hour, shrieking in a cracked high-pitched voice much too loud for its skinny body. The Mexican soldier had said they might as well go back to the camp, as the stilt had warned everything in the area that the hunters were there. Impressive as this was, Kevin was told to come back to Copano in the winter months and hear the great-voiced whooping cranes. The whooping crane's call was vibrant and deep-throated, echoing out of the marshes as if the land itself were voicing some lament. The description reminded Kevin of those lonely tales about men who had heard the banshee's wail, which folk said sounded as if the hills themselves were weeping over some great loss.

All of the Irish were wary of the marshes though, even if they did not have to hear whooping banshees at this time of year. For a while, no one had seen a snake of any description. Soon after their arrival at the mission, how-ever, some of the children who had been climbing on the walls came screaming back to the general camp about several dragon-like things they had seen. The men grabbed their guns and ran off to investigate. Soon they could be heard blasting away. Afterwards they had come back with the golden patterned bodies of several rattlesnakes, two of which were over six feet long. It was no wonder, Kevin thought, that the children had called them dragons. They looked just like the picture of Satan below St. Michael's horse in the priest's missal book back home. At the sight of them, Mrs. Donohue, among others of the women, fainted dead-away.

"It's no more frightened you were than I," said Mr. Donohue as he revived his wife with a wet cloth and a sip of whiskey. "I thought sure I was going to die right there when I laid eyes on those serpents of hell. God bless St. Patrick for saving our Isle from such monsters."

Looking at the snakes later, and with a colder eye, Rose's comment had been, "I wonder however it was that Eve could have trusted such a vile thing?"

Similar frights occurred until even the Irish began to

realize that all the powder and shot in the world would not rid Texas of its snakes. "Unless Saint Pat himself were to be coming down," said Mrs. Donohue, "and driving these hissing devils into the sea, we'll never be rid of them. It's not a heathen land we've come to, thank God in his mercy, but its creatures are in sore need of some preaching."

Kevin agreed. The snakes on the mission wall had been lazily sunning themselves—relatively still and hardly threatening. But it was a different story in the wild. Kevin learned to listen for the telltale rattling and hiss when he walked in the meadows and forests and became almost used to occasionally seeing a snake slither across the path in front of him or, more rarely, to come upon a coiled rattler sounding like a drummer with a twitch. In the marshes and bayous, one had to be even more careful. In such swampy places huge cottonmouths could scare the daylights out of a man when he noticed one of the silent, dark olive-brown vipers hanging inches away on a low tree limb.

And there were things other than snakes in the water. Tom almost shot off his foot the first time he and Kevin saw the still eyes of an alligator peering at them from the "log" Tom was about to step on. By sheer accident Tom had shot the monster through the jaw. The alligator wriggled quickly backwards into the reeds, but Kevin reloaded and put a bullet between its eyes. It was more than a few minutes before either boy could work up the nerve to step into the water and retrieve the beast. Finally they managed to haul it out on dry land and then rushed back to the mission to tell of the adventure. Later that day some men brought the alligator back to camp in an oxcart. There was a sort of hysterical curiosity which obliged almost everyone to touch its rough hide and peer at the long rows of teeth. It was a long time before the Irish, men or women, began to feel at home with such creatures. There were those among them who said a prayer to Saint Patrick and sprinkled their cabins with holy water against snakes every night for the rest of their lives.

Kevin was not on speaking terms with any of the reptiles, but found them more a nuisance to his ramblings than anything else. He remembered the tale of St. Kevin at Glendalough—how wild boar, eagles, wolves, and even the speckled trout would gather at his cell to eat out of his hand and listen to his words—and Kevin felt that his saint was watching over him among the wild creatures of Texas. What did bother him, and everyone else, were the insects. Flies they could stand, as there were flies even in Ireland, but the huge Texas mosquitoes were something new and terrifying. Everyone had so many red welts on their arms, necks, and ankles that it looked like the colony consisted solely of pox victims. The only thing that kept the mosquitoes away for a while was the rain, and the rain only made it more humid when the sun rose with its fierce heat.

No one was entirely healthy during their stay at the mission, and a few became so disconsolate that they simply packed up and left to find more hospitable lands. The rest seemed resigned to whatever fate God had assigned them in the new land and endured the situation as best they could. They were rewarded in early July with the arrival from Mexico of José Jesús Vidaurri, the Mexican government's commissioner over the colony. There was a perceptible change among the colonists almost overnight. No longer were they wayfarers in a strange land. They were citizens, soon to be homeowners, farmers, ranchers, merchants, and artisans.

*Chapter 10*

# A New Home

Soon after his arrival, Commissioner Vidaurri had organized a surveying party under James Bray, one of the colonists. Brian Ruadh was the first boy to sign up as a chain-bearer but was rejected in favor of older boys. It was Kevin who told him to go back and tell them that he could do the surveyor's arithmetic for him while he got on with the sightings and such. This caused no end of surprise among those who had journeyed from Liverpool on the *Prudence* with the red-headed lad. They knew him as an often lazy boy with the annoying habit of playing his tin whistle, not very well, at all hours and getting into all sorts of mischief. When Brian spoke up, James Bray had simply given him a pen and a piece of paper and said he must prove it. The question of Brian's ability was settled after a few minutes. The commissioner hired him on the spot as secretary to the surveyor of the colony of Refugio.

Kevin was interested in the surveying project, but found that he would rather just wander the countryside, exploring and learning all he could about its inhabitants, whether plant, animal, or human. Already he had picked up a good deal of Spanish, which made asking questions easier as the only people around who knew much about the land were the Mexicans. While Brian was busy marking off the town proper, Kevin, Tom, and Mr. Donohue visited various spots Kevin had located which he thought likely locations for a good farm. Having thought about it for over six months, Kevin knew just what he was looking for. It was a spot that combined safety, a source of water, well-drained pastures, a source of timber and firewood, and a pleasant view.

The trouble was that Kevin had found two such locations. Northwest of the old mission about fifteen miles there were two low hills which crested about two miles apart. Each was crowned with a *mata* of oaks, some quite large for the area. About halfway down each hill there ran a ring of limestone which with a bit of work would form an admirable terrace for an upper field. The lower fields sloped even more gently down to a wooded *galeria* along a small swift creek.

"I've been up one and then the other of these hills, Mr. Donohue," Kevin said as they looked out over the prospect, "but I cannot make up my mind which would make the better farm for you."

"For me, do you say?" asked Mr. Donohue. "Have you been out all these weeks looking for a spot for myself?"

"Of course he has," said Tom. "And what else should he be after looking for?"

"Why, your own spot of land, you thick-skulled rascals. But better yet," said the older man, "since Kevin lad has found us two of the finest parcels of land in Texas, and side by side no less, I'm all for taking whichever hill you're not after building a house on."

Kevin did feel a bit thick-skulled, but he had always assumed that he and Tom would work for Mr. Donohue for a year and then go off looking for their own place. This was perfect.

"The choice is yours, sir," said Kevin. "Where is it at all that you'll be making a home from this day?"

"I'll not be making such a choice," said Mr. Donohue, "lest it haunt me someday that I chose the better site. Kevin lad, throw a bit of dust in the air and see which way it falls. Whichever way it falls will be your hill. Go with the wind, Kevin Dolan."

There really was no wind, but merely an occasional shifting of the heavy humid August air which was barely sufficient to stir a leaf. Kevin scraped loose some dirt and pitched it straight above them. Mostly it came down on their hats, but just a bit drifted down the hill on some invisible breeze. Tom and Kevin looked across the shallow valley to their new home. There was a fresh wind tossing the trees on their hill, which was working its way toward them, making waves in the summer grass.

"God's grace, but won't Mary be proud," said Tom.

"Aye, and Stephen Patrick and your mother," said Mr. Donohue, "God grant that they get to see it someday with less trouble than ourselves."

Two days later Mr. Donohue presented himself, accompanied by Tom and Kevin, before Commissioner

Vidaurri. Formalities for the granting of land included presentation of a testimonial of good conduct and morals, a profession of the Catholic faith, and a statement from the impresario stating that he was willing to allow the applicants to settle in his colony. These papers were all in order, and Kevin watched with something like awe as the commissioner recorded their grant in the colony's *Libro Becerro*, a large calf-bound ledger which recorded the boundaries of all the grants and deeds in the colony. In early September, Brian came to tell Kevin and Mr. Donohue at the mission that they could begin moving. Their grants were to be surveyed that week.

Almost all of the possessions in the *Sea Lion* had been lost; the *Wild Cat* had fared better. In fact, there was little that the boys packed onto oxcarts that day which they had not put on Mr. Donohue's wagon nine months before. Mr. Donohue had no money left at all, but he had furniture, kitchen utensils, and farm tools—which in Texas constituted real wealth. It took three days for the sluggish oxcarts to reach their new homesite. It was a pleasant journey both because of their destination and the fact that

a sudden cooling of the weather had driven off the mosquitoes for a time. Rose and Mrs. Donohue were enchanted when they finally came over the top of their hill.

"Sure it'll look like Ireland in the spring," said Rose, "but I'm mightily glad we brought along these two great lads to be doing the haying and plowing and such. It's a great lot of land to be all under the hand of one man."

"Rose," said Mr. Donohue, "I've been putting off telling you this for a while, but I'll be telling you now. When we've done plowing the garden plot, there's not a male foot will be put in it. We men have trees to cut and houses to build and fields to plow and plant. We've no time for such truck as pulling weeds in a wee bit of garden as you used to talk me into doing."

They all laughed. Back home, as Kevin recalled, everyone had considered Rose a rather sickly spinster. Not only had she survived their long travels, she had positively thriven.

"There better not be any clumsy-footed plowboys in my garden then," Rose responded. "I'm twice the maid I used to be, you'll see."

And they did see. No one knew how long the growing season would last, but they all pitched in to get the ground ready and planted lest they be forced to eat nothing but meat and nuts all winter. They planted Indian corn, potatoes, and cabbage, and saved their other seed for a less risky spring planting. While this was going on and while they worked on the house, they all lived in a tent attached to one of the carts, much as they had beside the old mission walls.

Building a house presented a problem, Mr. Donohue pointed out. It had to be finished before winter and yet they had too little time to build anything more than a hovel. Kevin suggested using adobe, like that used in the old mission, but Mrs. Donohue did not want to be reminded of that crumbling ruin.

"Besides, Kevin," said Tom, "we haven't the time to be making the thousands of bricks it would take to be building a fine sort of house for Mr. and Mrs. Donohue. And what at all do you know about the making of adobe? I hear if we mixed it up all wrong, it could turn to mud around us."

"That's true," said Kevin. "I'll have to be studying more about it. But what about sod for now—like our house back home?"

"It's the wrong kind of earth, Kevin," said Rose, "and besides the whole house would be alive with creeping and crawling things. Adobe sounds good for the spring, or better yet limestone from down the hill—though I see precious little fieldstone about—but we need a shelter now. You've seen how the weather changes here. No doubt we'll turn twice around and be snowed upon unless we get something up soon."

"I saw the remains of a picket sort of house in Refugio," said Mrs. Donohue. "It was all plastered with mud to keep the wind itself out of the chinks. I surely don't fancy the notion of living in such a place for more than a season, but I think it would be easily put up."

That was obviously the answer, as the other colonists had discovered, and they began working on it the next morning. It was a far cry from the pictures Kevin had seen of American log cabins built of perfectly straight timbers thirty feet long, but there were no such trees in this part of the world. On their hill there was one large pecan tree and a fairly large oak. Both would provide shade for the house in the summer, but neither was very straight. There was plenty of wood around, but little of it could be used to build anything unless they sawed it into boards. Kevin could feel the blisters on his palms as he thought of the prospect of sawing the boards for an entire house by hand.

The idea behind the picket house was simple. First Kevin and Tom dug a trench where the walls would be while Rose and Mr. Donohue went searching for saplings of the right length. When cut, these were placed upright in the trench along with pieces of dry cane. The trench was then filled in and hammered down. They all carried water for a week to make enough mud to plaster the walls with, and there were plenty of jokes about Kevin's idea of a "close" water supply. Kevin had no answer to that, as digging a well seemed harder work than carrying the buckets of water. It was mid-October before the roof went up, after which Kevin had some time to explore their new farm more completely.

The humidity and terrible heat of the summer had given way to warm afternoons and cool nights. Rains came sweeping in off the Gulf with winds that put their palisade and plaster walls to the test. While there was no denying that there were plenty of drafts in the one-room house on the hill, everyone was delighted that there were so few leaks from the rain. When winter did come, they could insulate the walls by hanging blankets against them. It was a pleasant time. The corn grew so fast you could almost see it move and there was a feeling of luck, of things going right at last, that everyone shared.

*Chapter 11*

# Karankawa Tom

The first thing Kevin wanted to do was to walk their property line all the way around. Kevin and Tom's land on the tree-crowned hill to the north went from the edge of the creek to about 500 feet over the hill and was about half a mile wide. They had only qualified for a small farm—and that was only because Mr. Donohue had not listed them as his dependents. Mr. Donohue, on the other hand, had had little trouble convincing the Mexican authorities that he would get a herd of cattle together by the next spring. Thus he had received a full league of land, a square with sides over three miles long. Through Mr. Donohue's influence (the authorities had been impressed by his wagon load of goods), Tom and Kevin had been given a five-year option on the league surrounding their farm land. No one else could buy it or be granted it unless they failed to establish a cattle herd in that time. The boys considered it already theirs.

Thus Kevin and Tom set out one morning on a walk that would take them two miles out to the property's edge, then some 20 miles around the perimeter of theirs and Mr. Donohue's land, and finally two miles back home. Since they were going to be exploring, they gave themselves a week to do it. Kevin took along a compass, paper, pen, and charcoal ink, and of course his rifle with powder and shot. They both carried knapsacks with blankets and clothes, a bit of prepared food and a skillet.

The weather was cool and clear as they walked side by side along the creek. After a while the creek broadened out into a slow shallow stream with a bottom of white sand and glistening pebbles. It was easy to see how the early explorers had believed the land to be rich in gold and jewels when even the pebbles in a creek such as this were so beautiful. The creek turned southeast so the boys crossed it without getting too wet due to several large stepping stones. After walking due east for a little over an hour—Tom judged that they had walked about two miles —he called out to Kevin, "Tie a bit of rag to this tree limb and we'll see how close we come to following the straight lines of your compass and how well we can judge the length of a mile. When we come back this way from the south, we'll know for certain how great a pair of numb-skulls we are in the wilderness."

"It's not like we don't know the surveyors' landmarks are out there," said Kevin, "but sure I don't see one around. There should be one on the line between Mr. Donohue's property and ours."

Just then Tom came upon an odd stack of flat rocks. It was the cairn marking the northeastern corner of Mr. Donohue's land.

"Look here," said Tom as he lifted up a few of the rocks. There was a piece of wood beneath the third stone with some writing and numbers on it. "We've only been walking the length from Da's house to the village and already we're a hundred yards off course. You'd best be steering us better from here on."

After that, Kevin took compass readings more often, sighting a landmark of some sort and then walking to it. Between these stops, they kept a slow but steady pace and by late afternoon they came upon the next surveyor's cairn. It was a good thing, too, as the sun was just going down. By now they had gotten used to the glorious Texas sunsets. Unlike the lingering evening twilight at the end of the day in Ireland, in Texas the sun seemed to fall into the earth in a quick burst of reds and bright pinks. This was followed by a period of twilight which lasted only a few minutes until the land settled into a deep dusk. A strip of crimson lit the western horizon for half an hour more, but it gave little light to the land. It was no time for two novices to be trying out their camping skills, so they decided to set up camp at once.

Gathering the driest wood they could find, Tom made a small fire in the lee of a fallen tree trunk. Next to the fire they made a tent out of one of their blankets and some sticks. Looking farther into their packs, Kevin brought out a loaf of bread wrapped in a cloth, some venison jerky, and their water bottle.

"Did you come this far in your ramblings, Kevin?"

asked Tom. "And do you know if there is a stream nearby?"

"No to both your questions. Is it out of water we are?"

Kevin looked up to see Tom listening to the slosh inside the jug. It was clear that they would need to find some water the next day. Things didn't seem too bad though. The bread was fresh and warm from having been at the top of Tom's pack, and the water was cool. The jug was wrapped all around with a layer of twine which they had soaked before leaving. As the water evaporated from the twine, it kept the liquid inside quite cool.

"You know, Kevin," said Tom as he lay back and looked up at the incredibly bright stars, "I never thought—after we'd gotten used to it of course—that I would ever get tired of jerky when we first had it aboard the *Prudence*. But I think I can honestly say that I'm after hoping never to have to chew another piece of it again in my life."

"Me too," agreed Kevin. "But you've got to admit that it's an amazing variety of food we're after eating since we came to these shores. 'Tuna' from the prickly pear cactus, wild onions, blackberries, not to mention all the pecans we've eaten. Then there's the persimmons coming on, and of course game is just everywhere."

"Amazing is the right word for it," said Tom, "especially that salad poor Rose put together yesterday. Who told her a body could be eating those weeds?"

Both boys laughed at the memory of Rose eating mouthful after mouthful of the bitter dandelion and poke-salad leaves to prove that, if she could eat it, it must be good.

"Well, we've still a lot to learn and that's for sure. But tomorrow let's be on the lookout for a good fishing hole. I think I'll have a hero's hunger by lunchtime."

This sort of chatter had become a nightly ritual with Kevin and Tom. They talked about the little things—food, the cabin, Rose's screams over every new bug, how the garden was faring—and left the bigger worries for the daylight hours. The chatter would go on until one of them finally would mention Ma and Da, their sisters, or Mary O'Reilly. Then it would get quiet as each fell into his own thoughts. Tonight it was Kevin.

"What I would really like," he said, "is some of Ma's soda bread—or the little sweet rolls she made for last Christmas with sugar on top. You remember? She cut little crosses on top of them and we ate the last ones on the dock at Wexford."

"Ah Kevin, it's so long ago. Sometimes I think that I miss them—Ma and Da and everybody—I miss them so much that I half think I'll just wake up there."

"I know that feeling," said Kevin. "I wonder if they ever got our letter."

After a long while, Tom said, "Mary will love the stars here. She was always one to be out naming the stars."

It had been a long day, and they slept a long and dream-filled sleep. They heard neither wolves howling nor coyotes yapping nor owls hooting. When the morning came with a cool wind out of the north they awoke as fresh as if they had been at home on their own cots.

Tom had hung their knapsacks from a rope tied to a tree limb a little way from their tent. Examining the tracks in the soft ground, they could tell that the food in the bags had attracted the interest of several different animals during the night. Still, nothing had gotten into them, so they breakfasted on bread and jerky, this time with only a few swallows of water to wash it down.

Tom pointed out that if they didn't run across some water, it might be a very thirsty walk to the upper end of their stream. A little after sunrise they set out due west, heading for the rock-strewn crest of a hill on the horizon. The land about them was pretty, but the travelling suddenly became difficult when they got into a range of low but steep hills. It was more a series of gullies or washouts, *arroyos* the Mexicans called them, warning that such places could be very dangerous in a sudden Texas storm.

"Not exactly the finest in arable land we have here, is it?" asked Tom with sudden sarcasm. "I don't know why I ever trusted you to go picking out our land for us, especially when you hadn't even seen it all."

All the good feelings of the previous evening vanished like smoke. Kevin could feel his brother's tension and his own anger mounting. All the times he had been told to go on home when Tom wanted to be alone with Mary, the times he had shouldered Tom's bag of peat and obediently walked off over the fields, Tom's cutting words about his dancing barefoot with Mary, all the times he had said Kevin was too young to do this or think that . . . it all boiled up at once.

"Listen, you know-it-all plowboy, these gullies are all over Texas. We're lucky these are out here on the back end of our property where they probably drain into the meadows between here and our hill. Besides, it was Da himself told me to choose our land; it's *my* responsibility, not yours, so just keep your tongue in your head."

"Da only said that so you'd feel like there was something important for you to do till you were big enough to help with the real work! Sure you didn't think he meant it, telling you to do all the figuring and such?"

"Of course he meant it, because the brains to be doing it don't happen to be in your head. I don't know what a fine girl like Mary O'Reilly sees in you anyway . . ."

Tom couldn't take that and in a flash the two brothers were rolling down the gully pounding on each other, kicking and pulling hair. Kevin was getting the worst of it because of his size, but he wasn't about to give in. By the time Tom finally pinned him down with his arm behind his back, he had given Tom two black eyes and plenty of bruised ribs.

"This bloody land's not fit to bring a lass like Mary to," shouted Tom, straddling Kevin who was face down in the dirt. "Admit it, it's good for neither crops nor cattle nor women. Say it! Say it!"

"Well," grunted Kevin, "it's certainly good for snakes." He motioned with his head to where a brown viper was slithering away from their struggle and behind some rocks. Tom sat still for a minute before he began to chuckle.

"Ah, Kevin, I'm sorry. I'm so wound up about Mary I don't know what I'm doing half the time. The land's fine, and I couldn't have chosen a better piece myself."

Kevin rolled over and rubbed his jaw. "It'll be a while before I can chew any jerky with these teeth," he said. "You've rattled them as loose as nuts in a bowl."

"For what it's worth, you're a lot tougher than I thought. At least I won't worry so much if I have to turn you loose on any Indians. But let's get out of here and see what this land looks like from the top of that hill we were heading for."

It took them over an hour to work their way to the foot of the hill where the series of *arroyos* ended. In another hour they had climbed to its summit and found a limestone boulder to stand on and look about. It was higher than they had suspected and they were able to make out a good many of the landmarks for a few miles in all directions. Away to the south—all their land if their option on it held—Tom and Kevin saw a broad and fairly level plain of grass. Perfect grazing land, just as Kevin had thought. Beyond the plain rose a hill which was either their own hill or one of the two or three around it. To the north there appeared to be a fairly substantial river, most likely the Rio San Antonio, judging from the dark green line of trees which meandered in and out of view. The *arroyos* probably drained off periodic floods from the river north of them.

"Kevin, lad," asked Tom, "did you know this was here at all?" Tom pointed out over the plain. "We could run hundreds of cattle in such a place."

"I hadn't much idea what exactly was beyond our own hill. I was looking for a place to build a house and make a farm—not to be making an empire itself. Can't you just see Da's face looking out upon all this?"

"We must be for bringing them over as soon as ever it is possible," said Tom. "And yet I fear their coming through the troubles we've had."

Just then they heard a horse's whinny. It seemed to come from the north or northwest. The boys stayed very still for a long while, shading their eyes from the noon sun and staring out at the space between them and the distant river. "Look there, Kevin," Tom whispered, "where that *galeria* begins." Then Kevin saw them too—three or four horses, lean and obviously wild. "I think it's time we started rounding up some of our stock," said Tom as he began moving down the side of the hill out of sight of the horses.

As they walked, Kevin tied a loop into the end of the leather lariat he and Tom had finished braiding out of strips of deer hide only a few days before. The leather rope was stiff and not very long, but it would have to do. At the bottom of the hill, Tom told Kevin to take up a position by a narrow track that ran through a small *mata* of oaks. Tom whispered that he would go around and try to drive the horses Kevin's way, as neither boy was capable of getting close enough to lasso one where they stood. Kevin sat down to wait.

It was a long wait. A dark roll of clouds had appeared in the north and Kevin could see without any trouble at all that there was rain in it. He could see the dark blue streaks beneath the building cloud mass. Just about the time he felt the first puff of cold wind, he heard Tom hallooing for all he was worth. Kevin got the lariat loop ready and peered out from behind the trunk of a large oak. Tom was out in a small meadow, jumping up and down, waving his arms and yelling. For a moment Kevin thought he must have been bitten by a snake, he was jumping around so, but then he saw two horses come bolting into the small wood. The horse in the lead was a big one and it made a thunderous drumming as it pounded up the deer path. Gathering all his nerve, Kevin jumped out onto the path and flung the loop at the tall horse's head. But as soon as the smart old mustang saw Kevin and the lariat, he reared up and slashed out with his front hooves. Kevin ducked just in time to avoid having his skull crushed and flung up the lariat again, blindly this time. It landed firmly around the second horse's neck. In half a second, Kevin—the rope tied around his middle—was being dragged out of the wood and up the hill. Suddenly, the horse turned and reared. Kevin rolled just as the hooves came down. Lying down was obviously not the answer to Kevin's predicament so he jumped up and pulled hard on the leather rope. Round and round they went, dancing over the hill, with Kevin hanging on to the rope as the horse tossed its head and tried to rear again and again. Finally Tom came running up and took hold of the rope so Kevin could untie himself.

"Tie it to whatever you can!" he yelled to Kevin.

"Right."

Together they worked the prancing horse closer to the oaks where they at last managed to tie the rope firmly to a large limb.

Kevin fell back exhausted. His pants were torn in a dozen places and cactus spines were visible all over him. He couldn't begin to count the number of bruises he had. Looking from Kevin to the mustang and back again, Tom said, "Whew, Kevin lad, you've taken a beating this day. But I'm as proud of you as I can be."

"I think," said Kevin with a groan, "that being a puppet to a mustang is worse than being beaten by my own brother. But sure there's some things about this business

of horse catching that we need to be after learning before
we go at it again."

Tom laughed and got down to picking the cactus
spines out of Kevin's thighs and backside. "Reminds me of
that time you fell in the thistle on the day we decided to
come here. It seems so long ago." Suddenly Kevin stif-
fened and looked around for his rifle. It wasn't there. He
tapped Tom on the shoulder and pointed. Tom turned to
see an enormous Indian, tattooed and painted with all
sorts of odd designs—flowers and stripes—and naked as
the day that he was born. One half of his face was painted
black and neither boy could interpret the grin that showed
a number of missing teeth. Finally the Indian said, "*Más
cuerda.*"

At first they didn't know what he meant—they were

surprised enough to hear him speak. "What'd he say?" asked Tom.

"*Más cuerda*, more rope," said Kevin beginning to laugh. "*Sí, sí*," he said to the Indian, "*mas cuerda*."

At Kevin's laugh the Indian sat down beside him and began picking out the cactus spines. He seemed much more adept at it than Tom, perhaps because his fingernails were so long and thick—more like claws, Kevin thought later. Soon enough the job was done and the Indian reached into a leather sack he had been carrying along with a cedarwood bow as long as the Indian was tall. Protruding from the sack were several long arrows made of cane with a round length of harder wood at the end where the arrows' feather fletching was affixed. From inside the sack he produced a couple of thick spiky leaves, one of which he broke open and rubbed all over Kevin's scratches and punctures. As sore as he was, Kevin's wounds felt better almost at once. He gestured that he wanted to look at the leaf.

"There is some of this growing back at the house," Kevin said to Tom. "If we get out of this alive," he added in Gaelic, "it will be very handy." To the Indian he said, "*Gracias*," and reached out his hand.

The Indian just looked at his hand, then slowly extended his own. Kevin shook it and again said, "*Gracias*." Finally the Indian got the idea and began shaking Kevin's hand for all it was worth. Kevin kept nodding his head and the Indian kept pumping his hand until they were all laughing. Kevin then pointed to himself and said, "Kevin." He repeated it several times, then pointed at Tom and said,

"Tom." At this the Indian grinned a very wide grin and said "Tom, Tom," and began shaking Tom's hand as furiously as he had Kevin's. Pointing to himself, the Indian, practically dancing, said "Tom, Tom *tambien*, Karankawa Tom."

At that both Tom and Kevin looked at each other, but kept up their grins. Karankawa Tom was the name of an Indian their Mexican neighbors in Refugio had warned them about. He was a known cattle thief, and suspected of being much worse. The worst thing anyone could actually blame him for, however, was stealing a cow now and then which he promptly traded for supplies of one sort or another, usually a bottle of tequila—a Mexican drink that made the very crudest poteen taste as smooth as clear water. That, and the fact that he was a smelly nuisance was all anyone could actually prove against him. If he was really the murdering savage some people said he was, Kevin decided, he was an awfully friendly murderer. But he *was* smelly—horribly so. Later they found out that this was from the combination of buffalo grease or alligator fat and dirt which most of the coastal Indians smeared on their bodies as a protection against insects. At the time, though, it was enough to know that life was more pleasant upwind from Karankawa Tom.

"*Ba'ak*," said the Indian and he pointed to the approaching storm, then to a group of saplings.

"What's that mean?" asked Tom.

"I don't know—to make something, I guess, whatever a *ba'ak* is. Maybe he means just get ready for the storm before it gets here."

"Well, that's a fine idea whether that's what he means or no. *Ba'ak*," said Tom, nodding to the Indian.

Karankawa Tom took a small axe from his sack and began cutting saplings and sticking the ends in the ground in a circle. Tom helped him as Kevin gathered firewood. The Indian produced two deerskins from his sack and laid them over the framework after he had tied the ends of the poles together in the middle. The skins only covered the windward side of the structure, so Tom pulled out one of their blankets and spread it over the top. Kevin put their things inside and started building a rock circle for their fire.

Picking up his long bow, Karankawa Tom shook it and then made an eating gesture. Kevin said, "I think he wants you to go hunting with him, Tom."

"Where's your rifle?" asked Tom.

"I think I dropped it when the horse came through the wood."

"I'll get it. But I really want to see him use that bow. I've heard they can shoot an arrow a couple of hundred yards."

"Tom, *tabhair aire*," warned Kevin—"be careful."

While they were gone, Kevin got a good fire going as it was getting downright cold. The rest of the time he spent looking at his new horse. The dappled gray mare had tired herself out but was still skittish, whether because she was tied or because of the coming storm, or both, Kevin didn't know. She wasn't very old yet—maybe two and a half—so she could be broken to the saddle with a lot less trouble than could a full grown horse. It had been foolish of them to try to get that big stallion Kevin thought now—

especially tied to the lariat as he had been. If this young mustang had almost killed him, surely the stallion would have. Besides, what would they have done with an old horse they couldn't break to either saddle or plow? Kevin was feeling more kindly toward the horse now and gathered up some of the tall dry grass. The mare seemed almost grateful as she bent her head and began munching. Still wary of her hooves, Kevin began picking the burrs out of her coat. "What'll I call you?" he mused to himself. "A good Irish name . . . or something Indianish?" Just then lightning flashed across the darkening sky. "That's it," thought Kevin. Then he said out loud, "*Teintreac*, that's what I'll call you. *Teintreac*—Lightning."

Tom and Karankawa Tom arrived back at the shelter with a freshly killed deer just as the rain began to fall. With a flint knife, the Indian began carving the deer—without cleaning it or gutting it or anything. He just cut off great chunks of venison and handed them around to Tom and Kevin who spitted the meat on sticks and began roasting them over the fire.

"Oh, Kevin, I'm sorry I forgot," said Tom. He handed Kevin a full water jug. "There was a little creek in that *galeria* where we first saw the horses. It's a parched throat I bet you have," he added as Kevin gulped down the water. "We've neither eaten nor drunk any thing since breakfast."

The water was delicious and certainly made them feel better while they waited for their venison to roast. Karankawa Tom had finished one piece raw while he roasted another. It was an interesting night. Tom and Kevin warmed themselves beneath a blanket close to the fire,

while the Indian lounged beneath a single skin—his own.
Later on he went out to dump the carcass of the deer
away from camp. When he came back he had the deer's
hide slung over his shoulder. Inside the shelter, Karankawa
Tom lay down and calmly spread the hide, still bloody in
places, over himself like a blanket. For an hour or so,
Kevin tried his best to communicate with the Indian using
his limited Spanish and gestures. He made little progress
in understanding the mixture of Spanish and the Indian
language used by Karankawa Tom, beyond learning a few
words. Finally neither the storm nor the Indian's alligator
grease stench could keep Kevin awake any longer. If
Karankawa Tom wanted to steal their horse in the night,
then that's the way it was. But just to be safe, Kevin slept
with both arms around his rifle barrel.

*Chapter 12*

# First Blood

Tom and Kevin found the surveyor's cairn with little trouble the next morning near the spring where Tom had filled their water bottle. The spring turned out to be the headwaters of the creek which ran diagonally northwest to southeast across their land and Mr. Donohue's. Except for the problems of leading a skittish wild horse, the walk south was an easy one, over a grassy plain dotted with *matas* of oak, mesquite, pecan, and other trees. They saw charred remains of other trees as well. This was probably why the grasslands existed here—a fire every few years kept back the brush and encroaching trees.

Of course, the two brothers talked of little except Karankawa Tom that morning. When they had awakened, the sky was clear and the air cold. In the space of a very few minutes, the Indian had cut himself a loose fitting vest and a pair of leggings out of his deerskins. Just as quickly he had made Kevin a pair of leggings too, laced up the

back with a strip of hide. Kevin and Tom had taken this to
be a parting gift, so they had given him an old butcher knife
from their knapsack. The Indian was delighted. He
weighed it in his hand for a minute, tossed it easily back
and forth from one hand to the other, then threw it with
all his strength at a tree some twenty paces away. The
"boiiing" resounded through the small woods and Karankawa Tom turned a wide grin to them. "*Bueno, bueno,*" he
said. Then he gave Tom one of his four-foot-long arrows
and they parted with many handshakes and grins.

    "I keep wondering why that stinky old coot was so
friendly to us," said Tom as Kevin lined up another landmark with the compass. "You would think we were long
lost family, the way he pitched in and helped fix you up last
night. And I thought the Karankawas were supposed to be
some of the meanest Indians around. Wasn't there a big
fight, a war almost, between them and the Mexicans only
a few years ago?"

    "I think it was about eight years ago because they
signed a treaty with the Mexican government in 1827,"
said Kevin. "But I'm after wondering the same thing, because it *was* a war and they say—well, at least Commissioner Vidaurri said—that the soldiers killed over half of
all the Karankawas left in that one battle. The Commissioner told Brian and myself that now there probably
aren't more than two or three hundred of them left along
the entire coast."

    "And once they were the most important tribe here,"
said Tom thoughtfully. "All this used to be their land."

    "Yes. They've had it out with the Spanish and the
French and the Mexicans, and they even fought that

pirate, Jean Lafitte. Of course, it doesn't help with them having a reputation for being cannibals and head-hunters —not to mention being some of the smelliest folk on earth."

"Well, that's a fact I'm sure no one has made a tall tale of—you could hardly be making more of the truth than the truth itself."

The boys laughed at that and then Kevin said, "But still, you know, the Karankawas have been at war with their bows and arrows against armed soldiers now for almost as long as we've been after the English. It's a wonder they weren't killed off long ago."

"If you'd seen the way he used that bow yesterday," said Tom, "you might think twice about that. I could barely bend it full, and he killed that deer at about fifty yards— with the arrow going clean through it and into a tree. I wouldn't care to be facing such an enemy at all, not even with your fine rifle there."

"I wouldn't care to face a man who can bury a butcher knife in an oak tree either. But still and all," said Kevin, "it reminds me of the farmers of Boolavogue going up against armed men with only their pitchforks."

"It does, it does," agreed Tom. "Sure we're not the only persecuted people on God's green earth."

Kevin began to recognize more and more of the land, the farther south they went. He had looked this area over carefully when looking for homesites. As he expected, they came at last to a small lake bordered on its far side by the dark edge of a substantial forest.

"Here's your fishing hole," he said to Tom as they led Teintreac down to the water's edge for a drink. "Brian

Ruadh and the surveyors must have had a time finding where to put Mr. Donohue's southwestern cairn—I imagine that it lies in the middle of that forest."

"It's surely a forbidding looking place," said Tom. "I'm not sure as it's quite the place to be leading a horse through either. Can't we just be for skirting the edge of it?"

"Oh, I've got no great desire to be getting lost in there either. It goes on for miles south, down to just west of Refugio. I never went very far into it. It's full of greenbrier and grapevines and all sorts of things I don't have names for. Lots of blackberries though, so it'll be a good place to come in the early summer."

Together, the boys netted a couple of large bass—as well as a fat black cottonmouth. The vicious snake was one of the ugliest things about Texas and it gave Tom and Kevin a good scare. It was a reminder that one shouldn't go wading out into green water that can't be seen through. The freshly cooked bass, however, soon took the boys' minds off the snake. Grilled over open coals with only salt for seasoning, it was a delicious lunch.

After working their way along the edge of the forest to the point where Kevin thought they should turn east again, they built a *ba'ak* and settled down for the night. Even though it took them twice as long as it had taken Karankawa Tom to build the rude shelter, they were glad of its protection. They had learned a great deal in a few days.

They had not, however, learned enough to avoid getting lost. They spent most of the next day looking for the southeastern cairn, wandering around in circles until nightfall. After turning north the next day, they came to the lower end of "their" creek where they relaxed and fished. Just before sunset, they saw smoke rising from the top of a hill off to the west.

"That must be from Patrick's house," said Tom, "and if you don't mind, I think I'd just as soon sleep at home tonight as spend another night on the ground."

"I'm with you. I could do with supper at a table and a hot cup of tea myself."

Shivering with the cold wind, Kevin and Tom were all but exhausted as they made their way up the hill. Kevin's stomach was growling loud enough for Tom to hear it and he was in mid-chuckle when he froze as still as a stone cross. Kevin could sense his fear and whispered, "What is it?"

Tom pointed farther down the creek. At the edge of the trees and clearly visible in the bright moonlight stood a group of eight or ten Indians, their horses tethered to the trees. They were talking in low voices and pointing up the hill toward the house.

"We better get to the house before they do," said Kevin in the quietest voice he could manage. Since there was no place to hide Teintreac, they hobbled her there and began to make their way up the hill, parallel to the Indians.

About half way up, the silence of that bright moonlit night was shattered with the high pitched war whoops of the Comanches. There was no doubt in Kevin's mind about who *these* Indians were. There was something bloodcurdling about the very way they moved. Their cries cut into one like a knife. Without thinking further, Kevin shouldered his long rifle and leveled it at a Comanche racing up the hill. The two-part explosion of the flint's spark in the priming pan and the belch of flame and white smoke from the barrel blinded Kevin for an instant, but he, nevertheless, found himself running. He reloaded the gun as he ran, just as the Spanish soldiers had taught him to do on the beach at Copano: pull the powder horn plug with your teeth, shake it twice into the barrel, stuff in a bit of wadding and drop in the ball. Out came the ramrod to tamp it all down and finally a bit of powder was shaken into the pan. Kevin cocked it and fired again just as they reached the top of the hill. From the door of the house, a flash came from Mr. Donohue's matchlock pistol.

Without really knowing how they got there, Tom and Kevin found themselves in the cabin. By the time Kevin had reloaded his rifle for the second time, there was not a sound from the Indians. After a long silence, the three men ventured out to see if they were truly safe. Under the full moon, they could see the small party of Indians making their way up the opposite hill, Kevin and Tom's hill. Tom took the rifle from Kevin and aimed it high, as if he were going to shoot a bird from the pecan trees on the crest of their hill. He fired and shouted out *"Mallacht na mbaintreach agus na ngalrach ort!"*—the old curse of widows and orphans. The sound of it echoed down the valley.

After they had tethered Teintreach nearer the house in a spot with plenty of high grass, the boys finally got to change into some dry clothes and sit down to the cup of hot tea which had sounded so good more than two hours before. Just then Mr. Donohue came in from outside. He laid on the table a bow, a quiver full of arrows, and a long-handled tomahawk. "Looks like you killed your first Comanche, Kevin," he said.

"Where is he?" asked Kevin going to the door.

"Oh, you've no need to go look at him, Kevin," said Mr. Donohue. "Sit down and drink your tea. We'll bury him in the morning."

"I just killed a man. I want to see what I've done," said Kevin, and he went outside.

He found the Comanche about fifty yards down the hill. There was little doubt that it was his rifle shot which had brought down the Indian since the effective range of Mr. Donohue's pistol was limited to about half that distance. Lying in a crumpled heap, the Indian didn't look fierce at all. In fact, Kevin could see that he was not much older than himself. Kevin got down on his knees and turned the boy over, straightening out his arms and legs and closing his eyes. The bullet, a wild shot at best, had entered the left side of the chest. Just a few inches, thought Kevin, and he would have just wounded the Comanche. It hadn't been necessary to kill him—it had been a small raiding party and they had been scared off easily enough by Kevin's unexpected attack from their flank.

"I'm sorry," he said. "Sure, I didn't mean to kill you."

"That horse of yours is going to be a deal of work," Mr. Donohue was saying to Tom when Kevin came in. "We've no hay laid in at all and the fence is only half done around the yard in front of the house."

After that, no one spoke until Kevin finally said, "Rose, this is pretty good tea, but what's it made of? Another of your experiments?"

"Red sumac it's called," she said, filling his cup again. "Drink it up, now. It's more likely to put you to sleep than wake you up like regular tea, and I'm thinking you'll be needing sleep right now more than anything else."

Rose was right. The long day's weariness seemed to fall on them all. None of them, Kevin thought, had stayed up this late since the night they had spent packing the Donohue's things after the party. How long ago it seemed now. Yet it had only been eleven months, for this was the last day of October.

"Tom," said Kevin sitting bolt upright in his bed, "is this *Samain* night itself?"

"Aahhh," said his brother sleepily, "I suppose it must be."

"Imagine that, the very night we'd be at home in Eire with the doors shut and fearful of walking abroad at all, listening for the wailing of banshees and the treading of fairies on the roof. Here we were walking as bold as heroes through a wild land in the dark itself under a full moon. Sure I'm glad I didn't think of it sooner."

"Now that you mention it, I'm glad I wasn't remembering it myself," said Tom. "But we've had more frights in the last few days than I ever remember in Ireland—wild Indians coming out of nowhere, pulling that snake out of the very water we were standing in, getting lost. We must be getting used to this place. But shisht and get some sleep. We've plenty of work to be getting at in the morning."

Kevin thought about all that had happened, and especially about the Comanche boy lying outside. "Tom," he said at last. "I don't feel much like a hero."

# Chapter 13

# Rumors of War

That November hung in Kevin's memory for years afterwards as one of the most pleasant and yet the most exhausting months of his life. The weather was delightful: chilly nights, cool mornings, and warm afternoons, over and over again. Tom and Kevin spent a good part of each day preparing the fields for their spring planting. They chopped down the few trees that stood in the meadow Mr. Donohue had chosen for his primary planting, burned out the stumps, broke the ground with a yoke of oxen Mr. Donohue had purchased, and cross-furrowed that with Teintreac. Finally, taking small patches, one at a time, they burned the grass stubble and upturned roots. By the end of the month, Tom and Kevin could look out on sixteen acres of their labor, sixteen acres of rich black soil just waiting for the spring.

Of course, preparing the fields was only a part of each day's work. There was the corral they built for Teintreac

and the oxen, a woodshed to keep their firewood dry—
and *lots* of firewood had to be cut. The larger tree trunks
were sawed into boards or rough hewn with an adze into
timbers a foot square. The green timbers and boards then
had to be carefully stacked and weighted down so they
could cure, or dry out, without warping.

Kevin's hands had at last grown used to the rough
work, as had his muscles. He could tell this in two ways.
First, the work itself became more enjoyable as he devel-
oped the muscles needed for it. Second, the rifle which
Owen Morgan had given him as a present when he was so
ill with the cholera—was it only last spring?—and which
had seemed so heavy, he could now handle with ease. He
could hold the long barrel steady at his shoulder for almost
a minute while waiting for a clear shot at a deer or a rabbit
or a squirrel.

One afternoon late in November when Kevin was hunting a couple of miles southeast of the farm, he saw a horse and rider picking their way beside the stream. From the rider's bright red hair, glinting in the afternoon sun, Kevin knew him at once.

"Brian," he called, "Brian Ruadh!" The rider spurred his horse as Kevin came running down the hill.

It really was Brian. Sitting astride a tall horse with a rifle thrown across the saddle bow, he leaned forward to take Kevin's hand. It was one of those simple gestures which spoke volumes. No longer a slightly pudgy lad with a tin whistle, Brian was now almost wiry. There was a sense of balance about him that indicated days, not hours, in the saddle, and a wariness Kevin recognized as that of the trappers and mountain men they had seen in New Orleans. This was certainly a different Brian. Even his language had changed. His voice no longer crackled with laughter behind every other word—it was taking on the slower, subtle rhythms of the frontier itself that came of going long periods of time without speaking at all.

"Kevin, lad," he said as he dismounted. "Kevin, how are you? It's been almost five months since I saw you last."

"You've been out surveying that length of time, I suppose?" asked Kevin.

"Well, surveying, and other things. Just traveling you might call it. But I'll save my tale for Tom and the Donohues. Are they all right? Healthy and all?"

"Surely," replied Kevin. "Texas'll either kill you or make a man of you. It's even made a man of Rose."

Brian grinned at this, but Kevin missed his old friend's

quick laugh. As they walked on to the house, Kevin pointed out all their work—the fields cleared and ready for
planting, Teintreac in her new corral, the woodshed piled
high with firewood and neatly stacked rows of board
lumber. The house itself wasn't much to look at, Kevin
told him, but it was snug and they had great plans for
building when they had sawed enough board lumber and
squared more timbers with the adze.

To all this Brian didn't say much, though Kevin could
see that he appreciated the work involved. Kevin wondered exactly what Brian had been doing all these months.
His hair was long and shaggy now, and hung over a Comanche's buckskin war shirt. Half of its fringe was gone
and its smell was akin to—if not as strong as—Karankawa
Tom's unforgettable odor. He also had on what appeared
to be the very same pants he was wearing when he had
ridden west. But they were patched now with roughly
sewn pieces of leather and scraps of mismatched cloth.
The pants were tucked inside a pair of high boots like
those worn by the Comanche Kevin had shot, with a single
strip of buffalo hide for both sole and heel. Brian called
them moccasins.

Everyone was delighted to see Brian. Rose and Mrs.
Donohue rushed about to set a better than average table
while Brian drank cup after cup of steaming tea—real tea
this time, the gift of Brian's saddlebags. All the while they
kept up a steady commentary on every item of his clothing
and how skinny he had gotten and how long his hair was
and on and on. Finally, after putting away a much larger
meal than anyone would have expected to fit in such a

small stomach, Brian began to tell of his adventures and the news from the world around them.

"Well, Brian," said Mr. Donohue getting down a bottle of rum, "this is nothing like your father's poteen, God rest his soul, but it is at least a familiar drink. Here's a toast to our wayfaring stranger. To Brian Ruadh O'Mallory, son of Brian, one of the best friends I ever had—may God watch over him in his ramblings and may the wind be ever at his back."

"Thank you, Mr. Donohue," said Brian, "though I'm afraid it's an ill wind as will be blowing this way before too long. It's one of the things I came visiting you for, to be telling you of the rebellion that's brewing."

"What?" asked Rose. "Here in Texas?"

"Do you mean there's to be war with Mexico?" asked Mr. Donohue.

"Heaven preserve the Irish," said Mrs. Donohue. We can't be rid of bloodshed even by crossing the wide oceans. Why on earth should anyone of us be going to war with the good Catholic country that's after giving us—giving us, mind you—more land than any Catholic soul in Ireland has owned for hundreds of years? I see no sense in it and I'll have no talk of such nonsense in my house, even if it comes from the mouth of my own sister's son."

"Now, Margaret," soothed Mr. Donohue, "the boy hasn't said who's to be fighting whom yet. Let him get on with his story. What do you know of it, Brian? Are we truly to be involved?"

"Well, the President of Mexico, Santa Anna, seems to have taken it into his head that he's the man to be rewriting the Constitution of 1824. In other words, he wants to be king. He ordered that all the individual states of Mexico disband their militias in favor of one central army. I heard from a sailor down at Copano only yesterday that almost all of southern Mexico is in revolt."

"And you think, if there is war there, it will spread this way?" asked Tom. "Is there any evidence of that happening?"

"All I can say is that there is a whole lot of talking going on—meetings and such. There were some troubles before we came, you know. Mexico closed all the Texas ports except Anahuac a couple of years ago, and they passed a law saying that there would be no more immigration from the United States because so many of the arrivals were just frontier rogues and most were only pretending to be Catholics. One such pretender is a lawyer named Bill Travis, who's running all over the place right now preaching revolution, saying we ought to be making our own country here with its own government."

"And doubtless it will be a Protestant government," said Mrs. Donohue. "I knew it was beyond believing that we could move to the edge of the western world itself and live in peace."

"I think these folk from the United States have as much right to immigrate here as we did," said Tom. "Sure they're rushing things, but that's the way things are to the north. I heard Mr. Power say that the United States is actually trying to *buy* Texas from Mexico.

"From what I could make out while we were at Refugio," said Kevin flatly, "most Mexicans—including our neighbors—tend to think of the *Norte Americanos* as a bunch of Vikings just waiting for an excuse to start up a war with Mexico."

"That's just how they feel about them," said Brian. "But even if it comes down to just selling Texas—why would they want to sell off a land as fine as this?"

"Well, enough of politics and revolutions and all," said Rose, "tell us what you've been about these last few months and where you came by such outlandish clothes. Is all the surveying done? Do you have any news of the folk that came over with us? We've been so busy putting things to rights here that we've heard almost nothing of the other Irish families hereabouts."

Except to note that Pegeen O'Grady had finally arrived overland from New Orleans in September, there was little news of the other Irish colonists. Most had, like themselves, been busily employed in putting up temporary cabins and preparing their land. Brian's own story, however, was a long one. He had left the surveying party in late summer to go exploring on his own, up the Rio San Antonio all the way to the bustling little town of San Antonio itself. From there he had travelled north with a group of men to see about some land on the Rio Guadalupe. It was a place of high hills and heavy brush. It was beautiful, yet far wilder than anyplace so near the coast.

Brian, too, had a tale to tell of the Comanches. One night, he told them, as the group had bedded down for the night, they kept hearing bird calls, whistles, and hoots that did not seem quite right for the place and the time. One of the older men, Juan González, thought that it was surely Comanches. They had posted a double guard on their horses and turned in for an uneasy night's rest. No one heard a thing, but in the morning they found one guard unconscious and the other dead—and all their horses gone.

Juan and One-eyed Charlie Smith (a pirate, Brian told Kevin later, who had been one of Lafitte's men) insisted on tracking the Indians and getting even. There were eight men, including Brian Ruadh, all well armed. It took two days for them to find the Comanche camp, nestled in a bend of the river. When they came on the camp, the men had spread out along a dry gully and watched until they were sure that all the braves were in the camp. Everyone picked a target and, at One-eyed Charlie's signal, all their guns blazed. After they had all fired about three rounds, there appeared to be no movement in the camp until suddenly—out of nowhere Brian said over and over—they were surrounded by whooping and screeching Comanche braves. Brian had watched as the men fell one by one all along the gully, the lucky ones transfixed by long Comanche arrows, others with their heads split open by tomahawks or war clubs. Brian had hidden beneath a bank as darkness fell, and stayed there until the middle of the night.

When he at last crept out, he found the dead Indian whose shirt and moccasin-boots he was wearing. At the time it had seemed a good idea to dress in them. Brian had thought that he might get away disguised as an Indian, though of course a disguise would have done him no good had he been caught, since no Comanche had ever had flaming red hair. Somehow he had escaped their notice, crawling for a mile or more in the pitch black of an over-cast night. Finally he could not stand it anymore and he had simply run for it. "I just kept my head down and the north wind at my back," he said. After several days, he had dragged himself into San Antonio de Bexar, where he slept for two days straight in a small inn.

"Then did you came straight here?" asked Rose.

"No, first I went to Copano, then up through Refugio to see if there was any work to be had with the surveying crew again. But that's after being finished for the winter. It's then I thought I'd come look in on all of you."

As brave and soldierly as it all seemed in the telling, Kevin was bothered by Brian's account of the fight. "When you attacked their village," he asked (hesitantly, for he had an idea what the answer would be), "were only warriors there?"

"Not at all," said Brian. "As old Charlie said, if we're ever to clear this land of such savages, there can be no sparing of the women and children. No, I'm sure they lost three or four times our number in the fight. Just wait till you face some of them painted devils, Kevin; you'll show no mercy."

"Oh, Kevin's already the great Indian fighter around here," said Tom, as proud as he could be of his little brother, pointing to where the tomahawk, bow, and quiver were hung. "He killed that one with a single shot in the dark—and himself running full tilt up the hill outside."

"Ah, Kevin," laughed Brian Ruadh, "we're comrades in arms then. If we keep this up it will be no effort at all to switch from killing redskins to redcoats. Won't we be the soldiers some day!"

Rose and Mrs. Donohue were horrified at Brian's exploits, though they were none too uncommon among wayfarers in Texas at the time. They insisted that the "poor homeless lad" stay the winter with them. Thus it was that one year to the day after Mr. Donohue's farewell party in County Wexford, there was again music in the Donohue house. Tom and Rose and Mr. and Mrs. Donohue danced to Brian's tin whistle, which he had never lost in all his troubles. Kevin tried to keep up using a flute made from a piece of cane, but the flute and the whistle were badly out of tune with each other, and besides, Kevin had little heart for it. Even the singing of the old songs did little to raise his spirits.

*Chapter 14*

# An Irish Christmas in Texas

It was a night of memories, both good and bad ones, and of hard thinking for Kevin. Maybe it was drinking tea all evening or just the excitement of seeing Brian Ruadh again, but Kevin found himself still tossing, well after the others had fallen asleep. There were so many questions in his mind that finally he got up, dressed and put on a coat, and went outside. It was not uncomfortably cold, so he walked down to check on Teintreac. The horse snorted in her sleep as Kevin came up to her. He combed out the long mane with his fingers as the sleepy horse nuzzled against him. Finding that he had brought her no sugar cane, gradually Teintreac grew still again. Kevin went back to the house and sat down on the split-log bench outside the door. Tom had been right, he thought, staring up at the sky. Mary O'Reilly would love the stars here. Ireland had its twilight, but Texas had starlight like no other place on earth.

What disturbed him most, he decided, was not the things Brian had said—they were common enough sentiments on the frontier and Kevin had heard them before—but his own reaction to them. His reaction was utter confusion. If Mexico's President became a tyrant, things could go as badly for the Irish in Texas as they had at home under the British, except that here a person could always just pull up stakes and move farther west. But that was what they had done in Ireland—and you couldn't continue to run from oppression whenever it appeared. He had never wanted to run from it, in fact.

In Ireland, things had been much clearer. None of the Mexicans Kevin had met in Texas were very happy with their new President. As for the colonists, the Mexican government had given them land, the right to local government, a chance to make something worth living for in this new land. Their Mexican neighbors had given them advice and hospitality, and loaned them oxen and seed. But what of these immigrants from the United States? It seemed to Kevin that they were coming to Texas with the idea of taking it away from Mexico already in their minds. He kept hearing about the "destiny" of the United States. There was a continent for the taking, and they meant to take it. That idea had a very British feel to it, for Kevin. It smacked of colonialism, of empire building; it was the kind of thinking that had made it impossible for an Irishman to vote or own land or even worship in his native country.

The most natural way of seeing it all for Kevin would, he knew, seem downright crazy to anyone else living on the frontier. It was a big country, an enormous country, with plenty of room for millions of people. But it was being created in a bloodbath. Of course, the Comanches had killed Brian's friends—the Indians could only see these white men as the same sort of invaders who had wiped out all but a handful of the Karankawas. Kevin had heard that when the Spanish had first come to Mexico, they had destroyed not just a single tribe, but a whole nation of Indians, who if they were not Christian, were certainly civilized. Mexico City, the soldiers at Copano told him, was a glorious place as large as Dublin and filled with ancient stone buildings when the Spanish had arrived 300 years ago. And those soldiers—they were just peasant farmers themselves who had been taken away from their farms and families to serve in the Mexican army—did they truly want to go to war with the Texans, or with the United States?

In Ireland, it was so clear who was the oppressor. But here, Mexico was oppressing both the colonists and its own Mexican citizens. The Texans were oppressing the Indians whose land this was to begin with, and it seemed clear that the United States was intent on killing every Indian who tried to hold on to a piece of land that a white man wanted.

Looking out over the dark, upturned earth of the fields which had recently been a source of so much pride, Kevin could see that even this small bit of land had been taken from Karankawa Tom's people. Civilized or un-civilized, naked or clothed, smelly or not, Kevin knew they could be gentle. He knew they had families and children

and that there were Indian boys out there just like Kevin,
dreaming of growing up to be great warriors who would
drive the white man out of their land.

Kevin had at first been envious of Brian's Comanche
shirt, but now the bullet hole in that shirt seemed a shameful thing; the tomahawk hanging on the wall seemed the
Comanche equivalent of Mr. Donohue's old pistol. But
how could he tell such things to Brian, or to Tom? Both of
them were in favor of making a new country here, it
seemed, whether it meant war or not. How could he tell
Tom that he, Kevin Brendan Dolan, who had wanted to
throw stones at every British soldier he had ever seen, had
suddenly found that in Texas they had become just like the
British? It was wrong to carve a home out of another
man's land, yet it had to be right to protect that home and
the people in it.

The sound of the door opening broke in on Kevin's
thoughts.

"Kevin?" asked Rose quietly. "Whatever are you
doing out here in the cold of the night?"

Rose sat down on the bench beside him and spread
her shawl over both their shoulders. "What's wrong, lad?"
she asked, and for a moment it was all Kevin could do to
hold back the tears. But it had to be sorted out, if it could
be, so he began to tell her what he was feeling and thinking. It all came out in a rather jumbled sort of way—just as
jumbled, in fact, as it seemed in his mind—and for a while
Rose just ran her fingers through his hair and rocked back
and forth.

"Ah, 'tis true what they say, that Eire is an island of
saints and scholars, priests and poets. Perhaps that is why

all the old heroes seem so outrageous—Cuchulain with his 'hero light' sprouting from his forehead and all. We're more thinkers than fighters, Kevin, and if the world thinks of us as fighters then it is only because we've had such a just cause all these many years."

"It is just that I feel like everything is slipping away," said Kevin. "This land—I love this land already—but how can I be taking joy in it, knowing that it's been purchased in blood and is likely to be so purchased again? About the only thing I am still certain of is my hatred of the British injustice that drove us here in the first place. And even the fleeing itself cost so many lives at New Orleans and in Copano Bay. Just our coming here seems to have put such fear of rebellion into the Mexican government that it is willing to come stamp it out with fire and sword before it is even started."

"Shisht lad. There's blood on the land, that's true, but that is always true in heathen lands. These tribes have been killing each other for centuries and perhaps our coming will put a stop to it. And I'm sure the Mexicans are levelheaded enough to stop this Santa Anna of theirs before he marches this far north. I doubt there will be any bloodshed of that sort."

"Oh yes, there will be. We're scared of the Indians and the Mexicans are scared of us, or at least they are scared of the *Norte Americanos* and they probably think we're all alike. It is just like when Karankawa Tom walked up out of nowhere that first time. If I hadn't dropped my rifle in catching Teintreac, I would have shot him without asking any questions, just like I shot that Comanche boy. We take horses off the open range—maybe the Indians think of that as stealing horses from them. Maybe they were just taking back what they thought was rightfully theirs when they took the horses from Brian's group. Maybe all the Indian attacks have something like that behind them. Mexico gave us land, let us become citizens even, so why shouldn't they be angry when people up here start telling them how to rule us? I'm so confused, Rose. Maybe . . ."

Rose had to calm him again, holding him close in her arms. "We're all so blind, Kevin," she said at last. "Do you know how the British get most of their soldiers? Sure I've heard they take men right out of a pub, with their families at home only a block away, or they use prisoners guilty perhaps of stealing a loaf of bread. They even stop merchant ships at sea and pull off any man they deem to be a British subject, whether or not he has papers proving otherwise."

"What are you getting at?" asked Kevin.

"Only that you can never tell who it really is behind a uniform, whether it's peasants, like you said, wearing the colors of Mexico, or a Highland Scot who'd much rather be in a kilt than in British red. But it's not just uniforms we can't see through, it's people's skin—like the black slaves they treated so cruelly in New Orleans, or the Indians Brian is so proud to have fought."

"But Rose," said Kevin, sitting up, "if I am to worry about who it is at all that's inside a British redcoat, how are we ever to be rid of them in Eire?

"I don't know, Kevin Dolan. I don't know. But the killing will go on, there as well as everywhere else in the world, until people start thinking about other people like themselves."

"It's a muddle I can't get out of," said Kevin.

"That it is, but it won't be bothering you very long if you intend to stay out here much longer. Come inside before you catch your death of the cold."

Before he went to sleep, Kevin lay looking at the rifle Owen had given him. It hung over his bed where it gleamed in the firelight. So often he had dreamed of shooting down redcoat after redcoat with the gun, like so many targets on a fence rail. It had been a comfort then, a sure sign that he would eventually do what must be done in Ireland. There was little comfort left in it as he closed his eyes, exhausted in both his mind and body.

December was as cold as November had been mild, and this new hardship kept any idea of Christmas cheer far from the minds of the six people living on the windy top of a hill in Texas. Only now did it occur to them that perhaps they should have built their temporary cabin in a more sheltered spot. A "blue norther", as they called it, had come whistling and howling down on them, dropping the temperature so fast that the few vegetables left in Rose's garden had frozen solid between lunch and when they remembered to collect them in mid-afternoon.

Snow fell that night and all the next day, making the landscape a single beautiful sheet of white. It also drifted up against the cabin's drafty walls, insulating them and keeping the inhabitants, happily, much warmer than they expected to be. Except for feeding the animals and bringing in firewood, everyone stayed inside most of an entire week. Kevin, Brian, Tom, and Rose had gone out for a while on the first day to throw snowballs and try sliding down the hill on a board, but their clothes were no match for the bitter cold and so they gave it up. Kevin had heard that in 1821 Galveston Bay had frozen solid enough for a bear to walk across it without breaking the ice. He wondered if this weather was cold enough for that, or whether Texas was capable of even worse cold.

The days inside were pleasant enough. Kevin and Tom carved flute after flute from cane they had cut and dried earlier in the year. Finally they managed one that was in tune with Brian's tin whistle. Tom had also hollowed a slice of tree trunk and stretched a piece of deerhide, scraped very thin, over it to make a *bodhron*.

Mr. Donohue spent his days making clay pipes. He had found a clay bank along the stream and brought some home months before. It had gotten so hard sitting on the floor beneath his cot that he had to pulverize it with a hammer and mix it with water before it could be used. He made pipe after pipe and set them aside to dry. Finally he put them into the ash bed of the fireplace and built a very hot cedarwood fire over them. Out of twenty pipes, about half exploded from air bubbles in the clay. It was an amusing day for everyone except Mrs. Donohue, as every so often a small pop would indicate that another pipe had perished. Mrs. Donohue spent most of her time sweeping up the embers that flew out of the fire with each small explosion. When it was done and the fire had died down, Mr. Donohue was rewarded with ten pink clay pipes. He lined them up on the house's one bookshelf—actually smoking them would have to wait since he had run out of tobacco in October.

With plenty of music from the boys and lots of food—venison steaks and bread mostly, but plenty of it—everyone's spirits were high as the snow began to thaw and they could open the doors again for more than a minute at a time. But it was the 17th of December before things had dried out sufficiently to risk travelling.

The giving of Christmas gifts was not a widely observed custom among the Irish, but Tom, Kevin, and Brian had decided that it would be nice to give Mr. Donohue something. They owed him so much. Of course, Rose and Mrs. Donohue couldn't be ignored either. But what to give them? They could certainly make them things—pot hooks or a new stool or something—but that seemed more in the line of the usual chores. If one of the women needed a utensil of some sort, she would simply ask one of the boys to carve it. If Mr. Donohue wanted a new fence, he would just tell them where to build it. So it seemed that buying something was the best course. Brian was the only one among the three who had any hard money, so he volunteered to go with Kevin to Refugio and see what could be found. Their excuse was that Brian had some leftover business with the surveying team that he needed to clear up and that Kevin was just going along for the ride. They were saddled and off early in the morning.

Refugio was a bustling little village now. Streets were marked off with stakes and string, there were some houses being built and many more temporary cabins similar to their own, and there was even a shop or two. Kevin and Brian tethered their horses to a pole set in the ground with a metal ring on top of it in front of a one room general store on Federation Street. Actually, it was more of a trading post than a regular store, and the items to be chosen from were few. Luckily for the boys, the choices were obvious, pipe tobacco for Mr. Donohue and a bolt of calico cloth for the women. Brian paid for them and they were on their way out of town in a few minutes.

As they were passing the last street—you could only tell it was a street because it had been cleared of trees— they were hailed by Pegeen O'Grady.

"Kevin Dolan!" she called from the wagon she was driving down the empty lane, "Kevin, I have two letters for you!"

The old tavern mistress looked as hale as she had ever been—none the worse for her trip through the swamps of Louisiana and the piney woods of east Texas. She jumped down from her wagon perch in a billow of skirts. "I'm sorry I didn't get these to you earlier," she said, "but I couldn't find anybody who was going up your way.

Then the snows came and there wasn't a soul stirring out any place. I've had them for over a month and, well, here they are." Pegeen fished up two letters tied together from deep inside a large bag she carried on a strap over her shoulder.

Kevin untied them and saw that one was from his parents and the other from Mary O'Reilly to Tom. "Thanks, Pegeen," said Kevin.

"*Sláinte*," she called out. "Do come down in the spring. I'll be opening up a small public house, if they'll let me," she laughed.

In high spirits, the boys galloped most of the way home.

They arrived by supper time and charged up the hill, shooting off their rifles and yelling merrily. Kevin was waving the letters in one hand and his rifle in the other. Even the horses seemed in a good mood after their run and pranced a bit more than normal as Mr. Donohue led them to the corral.

He came running back saying, "What is it? Who are they for?

"I haven't read them yet. We rode straight back," said Kevin.

"Oh, how could you stand it?" said Mrs. Donohue. "I would have read them on the spot, whether they were for me or not."

"Oh, Ma," chided Rose.

"One is for myself and Tom from our folks; the other is for Tom alone, from his sweetheart."

Of course, a great production was made of reading the letters. The Dolans sent all their sympathy for the loss of life and the hardships everyone had suffered, but were overjoyed to hear that their sons had come through safely. The letter was full of news about Brigid and Cathleen— how pretty they were getting, how tall they had grown, and how well they could do their lessons. Michael and Peggy and their little Stephen were all well, as was Christopher, their newest arrival.

At the end of the letter there was an added note: "We don't want to spoil the surprise, but the letter to which this is attached has our complete blessing."

At that, Tom, who had been eagerly fingering his letter throughout Kevin's reading, tore it open and scanned it quickly. Everyone could see it was a joyful letter, but Tom let out no yells. He simply leaned against the wall and said, "I can't believe it. The lass is coming; she's already on her way." He looked again at the letter. "They sent the letters on a ship that left Wexford on the 10th of August, just a few days after they got our letters. Then Mary was to take ship on the 15th day of September." Tom looked up truly alarmed, "Then where is she at all?"

Tom had been rather moody, Kevin had noticed, off and on for the last several months. He had expected a letter long before this, and had tried to work off his worries in plowing and cutting wood. The amount of work produced this way was impressive—but it had given Kevin an often-too-silent partner. Now Tom stalked out of the house and stood in the middle of the yard, staring out into space.

"Sure, he's probably praying," said Kevin, "but there's no need to freeze himself to death doing it." Kevin took his brother's leather jacket and his own off the pegs by the door and went out to join Tom. Together they began walking down the hill toward the creek. For a long time, they walked in silence. Finally Kevin said, "Thomas Dolan, if you're not after talking to me about what's bothering you now, I'll put off speaking to you again until next year's harvest. Truly you haven't said two words to me at all since our walk around this land in October, except to say fetch me this or that. But I'm your brother, so talk to me."

"Oh, I'm that sorry, Kevin lad. It's just that I've been out of my mind this last month thinking maybe Mary had taken up with another fellow, or had just lost the loving of me somehow. I couldn't put words to my fears, but now I find she's been travelling here through the length of time I've been so worried. Where can she be, Kevin? By anyone's reckoning she should have arrived weeks ago."

"By anyone's reckoning," quoted Kevin. "What sort of reckoning is there at all in travelling to such a far place as this? She'll get here in her own time as weather and ships and coaches permit. But cheer up. She must love you mightily to be coming all this way for a wedding that's not even had any banns published yet."

"Kevin, you do cheer me. But it's that worried I am still. Anything could happen to a young lass travelling alone."

"You'd be better off figuring out what you'll be doing with a wife—and babies no doubt—if that cracked President of Mexico actually intends to make war on us here."

"Yes, I've been thinking on that as well. Rose is after telling me that I ought to talk to you about that and I told her, 'Rose, that boy has a true Irish rebel's heart. What should I be telling him?' And she just says to talk to you. What is it that's bothering you, little brother?"

"I'm not sure I've got the thing sorted out enough to make any sense of it to you. Basically, I guess it is just that we came here to live peacefully in a Catholic land, to escape being destroyed by the English. And here we may have to side with either a Catholic government that's been none too gentle to its own people or with a bunch of Protestant invaders, most of them with English names. I'd just as soon side with the Indians except we're standing on land that was stolen from them. Make sense of that if you can."

"Kevin, lad. You must remember that you're not the only person with a head on your shoulders or a heart in your breast. Don't you think we've all had the same thoughts? As to the Indians, I haven't killed any and I don't wish to be doing so. If they must be our enemies, though, the best we can do is to try and protect ourselves and, like Christ said, love them when we can."

"I don't think that is what our Lord said, exactly. But what about Mexico and this revolution or war or whatever it is to be?"

"What I think is that I'm not going to think a lot about it until I hear something more than Brian O'Mallory's version of things. His Da was full of tall tales, and I don't doubt but that some of this latest blather has been stretched a bit at the corners. If it hasn't, we'll soon find out. When we do, we can be making that decision—you and I—not going off half-cocked like Brian."

It was not a crystal clear solution for Kevin, but it would have to do. Kevin wondered how Rose had come to be so sure of things, but then Rose had changed a great deal in the last year. From a laughable old maid tending her father's garden, the butt of rude jokes, she had become someone to admire. She had proven herself kind and loving and strong. Perhaps it came from simply enduring what they all had endured.

The injustice that so angered Kevin, from their being driven out of Ireland to the dilemma of who was oppressing whom in Texas, was all very human in its origins and it was up to humans to work it out. But what of the deaths from the cholera? What of Brian's parents? Kevin remembered the afternoon in New Orleans when Brian had questioned the injustice of his parents' deaths. Why had God allowed them to come so far if it was only to die? Rose had said at the time that there was "no answer." And now Mary O'Reilly was stravaging about in this land somewhere. Or maybe she was shipwrecked, or dying of some disease, or murdered by Indians.

Obviously, Kevin decided, this was a problem for a scholar—or a saint. It was like the Lord's prayer, where you prayed for specific things—for daily food, forgiveness of sins, protection against evil—but at the same time you told God that it was what He wanted rather than what you wanted that was important. If Jesus Himself had to die on a cross, maybe the business of life was simply unfair from the beginning. Kevin didn't like that answer either.

"Tom," he said at last, "do you remember the old stone cross and the time we prayed up there together?"

"Sure I remember. You prayed for rain and we got drenched before we got home."

"And you got your Mary that day as well." Tom was

silent, so Kevin went on. "There's no stone cross here, but maybe we could walk up our own hill yonder and be saying some prayers for Mary in her travels." Tom gave Kevin a quick hug and nodded.

From the top of their hill, Kevin half expected to see Mary riding up the creek. There was a wind tossing the trees and a bright afternoon sun low in the sky. Across the valley they could see all their labors laid out before them— the house and woodshed tiny specks atop the opposite hill, the plowed acres of rich brown earth dark against the waving fields of golden winter grass surrounding them. And there were patches where the bluestem grass had gone almost orange. It was one of those moments when you could feel the earth sleeping beneath you and the power of it building toward spring.

After their prayers, the brothers stood looking out across the valley for a long time. "It's a good land," said Kevin simply, and they went down.


On the morning of Christmas' Eve, the countryside was once again frosted with a light blanket of snow. Since the boys wanted the Donohues to enjoy themselves as much as possible on the day, they had left their presents on the table the night before. They had been awakened by Mrs. Donohue's screams of delight when she found the bolt of cloth. Rose was equally delighted. Mr. Donohue said that he would wait until after breakfast to smoke his pipe, but he kept smelling the tobacco and fingering one of his homemade pipes throughout the meal. Finally Brian

Ruadh surprised them all with one more gift. He placed two small bags on the table—one of sugar and one of coffee. Before long the house was filled with the rich smells of freshly brewed coffee and sweet breads baking.

Altogether it was as fine a day as Kevin could remember. While Rose and Mrs. Donohue spent the day preparing for the Christmas "feast", everyone else sat around while Kevin read from Mr. Donohue's Bible. But as the day went on, Kevin could see that Tom was growing worried again. Finally, late in the afternoon when the light outside had gone all pink and orange from the sunset reflecting off the snow, he said, "I was sure that my Mary would have arrived by today and been able to light the Christmas candle." It was all he could say, though everyone saw that he felt like screaming inside.

Kevin eased things by saying, "Tommy, perhaps you haven't noticed, but we haven't got a window to be putting a candle in, and sure we're not going to sit here with the door open all night."

Tom smiled a little at that, and then he perked up. "A candle's no good in this wilderness at all," he said. "But let's build a good Irish bonfire on top of this hill to let all the birds, beasts, Indians, and whoever or whatever else is out there know that we know what this night is."

There was no doubting that a bonfire was just what was needed, even if it was a waste of wood. Everyone put on their jackets and pitched in, stacking up branches and split logs until it was as high as Kevin's head. Tom got a firebrand from the fireplace and carried it outside to Mr. Donohue.

"Patrick Eamonn Donohue," he said, "would you be doing us the honor of lighting this fire? It's our very own lives that we owe you for bringing us to this new land. Now bless us with a prayer over this fire, and then go find what's left of the rum."

Everyone laughed to see Tom in such cheer, then grew quiet as Mr. Donohue took the burning branch. "For the Mary that bore our Savior this night," he said, "and for the Mary that is to come and abide with us." Crossing himself, he pushed the branch into the kindling at the heart of the bonfire. Within a few minutes, the flames were shooting higher than the house. Around the crackling blaze they sang Latin hymns and Gaelic carols with Brian, Kevin, and Tom whistling, fluting, and drumming along. The night had gotten pitch black around them and they were singing so loudly that they didn't notice Pegeen O'Grady's wagon coming up the hill until it was at the edge of the circle of firelight.

"Halloo," she cried. "I see the Irish here still know how to let a body know where there's a *ceili* going on. Sure we'd still be lost in these hills if we hadn't followed your bonfire like a beacon from Tara itself."

"Pegeen," said Margaret Donohue, "welcome to this house. But who is it at all you've brought with yourself?"

Everyone looked to the wagon then, only to see Tom and Mary O'Reilly locked in a long kiss. Slowly they pulled apart and looked at the happy faces of the circle of friends. Then, all at once, there was a commotion as everyone tried to hug everyone else, and all tried to hug Mary. Kevin buried himself in her arms, knowing that this was a true beginning for both Tom and himself. It was a beginning in joy—not marred by sorrow or shipwreck or dilemma. At last she held him out at arm's length, hands cupping his face. "Well, tell me, Kevin lad," she asked with a bright smile and the firelight in her hair, "have you learned to dance with your shoes on in this new land?"

Whatever had gone before, thought Kevin as he watched Tom and Mary dance in a circle round the fire, this makes it all worthwhile. Stepping out of the firelight, Kevin looked up at the incredibly bright stars, then across the valley to their hill—his and Tom's and Mary's. As if some of the starlight had strayed before his eyes, he saw a line glistening down the black mass of the hill. "Saint Kevin's path," he said to himself. He bent down and picked up a smooth round stone, like a cobblestone. And put it in his pocket.

# Historical Note

Some readers of this novel have been concerned over the amount of history it contains—history that American readers probably never have encountered. This is a very real concern. Many college students majoring in European history will never study a single page of Irish history, ancient or modern. Thus we are so often mystified by the "troubles" as they are called in Northern Ireland, and aghast at the actions of the Irish Republican Army.

The fact of the matter is that the English have been invading Ireland periodically ever since the Norman Conquest of Ireland in 1070-1071. In the year 1607 occurred what is called the "Flight of the Earls." Under great pressure from the English, several of Ireland's most distinguished leaders went into exile. Two years later, England introduced into Ulster (Northern Ireland) several thousand English and Scottish Protestant settlers, the Irish Catholics in the county having been evicted by force. The last of the "Four Masters"—some of Ireland's best historians—wrote that it was at this moment that "the race of the Gael . . . passed under a cloud of darkness." The cloud lingers to this day, though it is not nearly so dark as it once was.

By the nineteenth century (when *With the Wind, Kevin Dolan* takes place) the penal laws imposed on the Catholics of Ireland were as oppressive as any such set of laws has ever been in any place. Irish Catholics were not allowed to worship (priests were executed, churches burned), to gather in any sort of group meeting, to own land, to hold political office, to vote, to make religious pilgrimages to holy sites, even to go to school. Thus when Kevin and his sister talk about school, they are referring to an illegal "hedge school," that is, a teacher sitting under a hedge teaching those students who wished to learn. This sort of oppression led to innumerable small revolts which were put down with such severity that their memory is still alive in Ireland today. The English atrocities during the Wexford rebellion in 1798, for example, remind one of King Herod's treatment of the infants of Bethlehem.

The effects of the English exploitation of Ireland eventually reached into the very soil of the "Emerald Isle." There was a time when Ireland was also called the "wooded isle." Virtually all of the large forests in Ireland, including the famous oak forests of Shillelagh, were cut and sold as timber in England. The primary source of fuel in Ireland thus switched from wood to peat, a very poor grade of coal. Wood became so scarce, in fact, that houses were made of sod and walking sticks were cut from a bush (the blackthorn) instead of Shillelagh oak.

Another concern of the initial readers of *With the Wind, Kevin Dolan* was whether a boy of Kevin's age would be so familiar with the history of his country. It is a characteristic of oppressed countries such as Ireland that the history of the oppression itself becomes a subject of obsessive interest, one that is taught almost from the cradle. What appears in *With the Wind, Kevin Dolan* is, in fact, a very small sampling of the sort of knowledge an Irish lad in County Wexford in the 1830s would have possessed.

Listed below are a few books used in writing this novel. Perhaps you will find them as interesting as I have.

Bancroft, Hubert H., *History of Texas and the Northern Mexican States*

Bedichek, Roy, *Karankaway Country* and *Adventures with a Texas Naturalist*

Castañeda, Carlos, *Our Catholic Heritage in Texas*

Dobie, J. Frank, ed., Texas Folklore Society, *Legends of Texas*

Doughty, Robin W., *Wildlife and Man in Texas*

Fehrenbach, T. R., *Lone Star: A History of Texas and the Texans*

Flannery, John Brendan, *The Irish Texans*

Flood, W. H. Grattan, *Introductory Sketch of Irish Musical History*

Huson, Hobart H., *The Refugio Colony and Texas Independence*

Irvine, John, *A Treasury of Irish Saints*

Newcomb, W. W., *The Indians of Texas*

Oberste, William H., *Texas Irish Empresarios and Their Colonies*

O'Connor, Kathryn Stoner, *Presidio La Bahia*

Power, Patrick C., *The Book of Irish Curses*

Smithwick, Noah, *The Evolution of a State, or Recollections of Old Texas Days*

Texas State Historical Association, *The Handbook of Texas*

Writers' Round Table, *Padre Island*

Yoakum, Henderson K., *History of Texas From Its First Settlement*

# A Glossary of Irish Terms*

*banshee (băn'shē)* - a female spirit; literally "a woman of the fairy hill" (*bean sidhe*).

*bodhron (bōr'ĕn)* - a drum, 2 to 3 inches deep and 18 to 24 inches in diameter.

*boreen (bōr ēen)* - a narrow country lane, often bounded by stone or earthen walls.

*caoine (kēn)* - the wail or cry of a banshee, or any loud lament.

*ceili (kāy'lē)* - a dancing party, outlawed at this time by the English, as were all such gatherings.

*colleen (kä lēn)* - an unmarried girl (from *cailín*, a girl).

*cullough (ke'lōw)* - to have lengthy conversations, usually at twilight, ranging from local gossip to current events to informal lessons in genealogy and history.

*curragh (kŭr'äh)* - a small boat made from oxhide stretched over a wooden frame. Used mostly in rivers and along the coast, but larger curraghs have been constructed which have crossed the Atlantic Ocean. See Tim Sevrin's *The Brendan Voyage.*

*Eire (ay'rĕh)* - Ireland.

*filid (fē'lē)* - a poet trained in the recitation (and the very complicated composition) of formal Irish verse.

*go mbeannuighe Dia annso (gū măn'nuēe dyēe'äh ăn'sŭh)* - The traditional greeting when entering a Catholic home in Ireland, meaning "God bless all here."

*hurly (hŭr′lē)* - (from "hurling"), a game resembling lacrosse, except that it is played with broad-bladed wooden sticks.

*oidhche na ceapairi (oi′chĕ näh kŭ′pay rēe)* - a traditional name for Christmas, meaning "night of cakes."

*poteen (pä tēn′)* - a whiskey made in a "pot still" and using a single type of malt. Outlawed by the English.

*ruadh (rū′äh)* - a reddish color.

*Samain (sä′wän)* - only roughly equivalent to Halloween, this is the night when fairies, elves, and other creatures and spirits walk abroad.

*teintreac (chain′trăk)* - lightning.

* These pronunciations have been derived from a number of sources, including American scholars, Irish musicians, and native speakers of Modern Gaelic. There is a remarkable amount of disagreement over how some of these words would have been pronounced in 19th-century Wexford, and even more in 19th-century Texas.